Deuce couldn't find his  the office to find Ace wai

"Trying to call you," A

"I can't find my phone." Deuce was in a panic. everywhere. Do you know what this means? I can't text Dani."

Ace looked at him incredulously. "You can't find your phone, and that is what you're worried about?"

"I have to set up a meet with her this weekend." Deuce shook his head. "This is so weird."

"Sorry about that, Bro," Ace said. "I hope you find it soon."

"Me too," Deuce said. "There is probably no need to panic. So how's it going? Dr. Jackson. How is Kiya? You two still in the nauseatingly lovey-dovey stage, aren't you?"

Ace laughed. "No need to sound so jealous."

"I am not jealous," Deuce said. "I was going to be in the lovey-dovey stage soon, with my mysterious text pal, Dani. But now, I can't find my phone."

"I actually thought that Kelsey would have gotten through to you," Ace said, "and that you would have forgotten about your text pal by now."

"Nope." Deuce walked toward his office, and Ace walked behind him. "If anything, seeing Kelsey recently strengthened my resolve to move on. And the best person to do it with is someone I've been talking to for the past year.

DEUCE

BRENDA BARRETT

JAMAICA
TREASURES

DEUCE

A Jamaica Treasures Book/March 2020
Published by Jamaica Treasures
Kingston, Jamaica

This is a work of fiction. Names, characters, places, and incidents are either the product of the author's imagination or are used fictitiously. Any resemblance to an actual person or persons, living or dead, events, or locales is entirely coincidental.

978-976-8247-74-2
Jamaica Treasures
P.O. Box 482
Kingston 19
Jamaica W.I.
www.fiwibooks.com

ALSO BY BRENDA BARRETT

ABOUT THE AUTHOR

Books have always been a big part of life for Jamaican born Brenda Barrett, she reports that she gets withdrawal symptoms if she does not consume at least two books per week. That is all she can manage these days, as her days are filled with writing, a natural progression from her love of reading. Currently, Brenda has several novels on the market, she writes predominantly in the historical fiction, Christian fiction, comedy and romance genres.

Apart from writing fictional books, Brenda writes for her blogs blackhair101.com; where she gives hair care tips and fiwibooks.com, where she shares about her writing life.

You can connect with Brenda online at:
Brenda-Barrett.com
Twitter.com/AuthorWriterBB
Facebook.com/AuthorBrendaBarrett

Chapter One

Some people are meant to be together, and I now know that you and I are destined to be....

Deuce read the first part of the message incredulously.

I was wrong and stupid to let us go.

Throwing away fourteen years of memories was foolish. Please can we meet?

Deuce reread the message and fought the urge to reply with a terse, *no*. He wouldn't entertain her; he would not respond at all.

Kelsey was writing as if they had just broken up, and she didn't have three years and marriage to another man under her belt.

So she was back. Good for her. And she was single and ready to mingle. As usual, he was her pit stop on the journey to finding herself.

This is how it has always been for them. They would break up, usually because of Kelsey's desire to see other people, and he would hope for her to come to her senses, and they would pick up where they left off when she claimed that she did.

When they had broken up the last time, Kelsey had sent him a similar text, except it had read, *some people are meant to be together, and I now feel within with my heart that it's not you and me. Dale Julius is the man that God has ordained for me, I hope you understand.*

Now all of a sudden, she wanted to give their relationship a try again. He felt resentful, but he also had a perversely happy feeling. She was no longer with Dale Julius, the other DJ.

He looked at the message again and wonder if he should respond. *How's Dale, your husband? Well, ex-husband, the one that God was supposed to have found for you?*

However, that would be showing some sort of emotion, and he did not want to reveal any of himself to Kelsey Channer Julius—freshly divorced from his best friend from med school.

He knew the marriage would not have worked between Kelsey and Dale. They had two vastly different personalities.

Dale was a quiet, and unassuming fellow, and Kelsey was an extreme extrovert who couldn't sit still, and always up for an adventure. Dale was not equipped to put up with Kelsey's dramatics. Only someone who loved her would put up with that. Someone who knew her from they were kids and loved her despite all of her quirks.

He was that person, had been that person, he corrected in his head, but he didn't know if he still felt that way anymore. What he felt for Kelsey now was more along the lines of apathy and indifference. Still, she was not in his vicinity at the moment, and her bid to win him back had just started.

He had been in this position before, where he thought he

had well and truly moved on, but she wheedled her way back in his life.

He got into his car, feeling thankful that for the next couple of months, and the foreseeable future, he would be working regular hours. His stint at the children's hospital was over, and he was back to his practice where he set his own hours.

His phone pinged, and he saw that another message had come in. He picked it up before starting his car. He wondered if it was a new text from Kelsey. He had no doubt that the message that he received this morning was just the start of her campaign to woo him back.

He wouldn't be surprised if she sent him a picture of her face with a tear in one eye. He wished there was some way to inoculate himself against her, because without fail, he would fall for her 'sorry I didn't mean it' story.

When he checked the message it wasn't a picture from Kelsey, it was a message from his text pal, Dani.

She had taken her clients on tour the day before.

He imagined that she was a tour guide of some sort, but he did not ask.

It was a picture of the sunset. A beautiful swirl of pink and red swaths surrounded the dying sun as it sunk into the sea.

He texted her back. *Where is this?*

Her reply: *Crimson Hills, Trelawny. It's a beautiful place. We picked up a passenger, still trying to figure out what to do with her.*

Interesting, Deuce texted back. *Who is this passenger?*

A woman running from something. Dani texted back. *She won't give us any information, had a cut on her forehead. We have a doctor looking her over. Are you a doctor, DJ?*

Deuce grinned. For all their going back and forth in the past year and a half, they were both careful not to give away specifics about each other.

Asking him if he was a doctor was a blatant violation of their unspoken rule— don't get too personal.

He didn't know if he was ready to meet her or if he even wanted to. His time with Kelsey had hit him hard, and he was still wary of getting close to anyone.

Technically, he knew that not all women were like Kelsey. He knew that it was not all drama all the time and that he didn't have to work so hard to protect himself from all the women he came into contact with.

He contemplated Dani's question. *Are you a doctor, DJ?*

Maybe it was time they changed the rules and found out more specific things about each other, including their professions.

Maybe she was the one who would break his Kelsey spell. The spell where he had found himself embroiled in thinking that Kelsey was the only one for him.

His fingers hovered over the phone for a while as he contemplated this next step. He typed in, *yes*.

And then, he typed, *what do you do?*

The die had been cast; he was moving forward.

****

Danica looked at the text and grinned. He was a doctor. It meant that they had moved along their relationship. Her next question should be what type of doctor, but maybe she was pushing too hard.

She texted back her response. *My official job title is recreation director, but I have too much fun to be calling this a job. My clients are delightful, and they are always up for an adventure.*

"Why are you stopping?" Stella panted. "Is it that text-pal of yours again?"

Danica looked at Stella, a smile playing about her mouth. Stella was now her regular hiking partner and lunch buddy.

She was looking at Danica curiously as she paused to stretch her legs on a tree stump.

Danica had now been working at Golden Acres for three months, and already she felt as if Stella was a good friend. She reminded Danica of her cousin, Elsa. They had similar personalities.

They had clicked from the moment that they had set eyes on each other when she went to Stella's office to be briefed about her new position.

They had lunch together that day and had lunch together ever since. They even lived beside each other in the staff accommodation.

"Yup," Danica said. "I just found out that he's a doctor."

"Well then that narrows it somewhat," Stella mused. "Did he say, medical doctor specifically or just doctor? If he said medical doctor, then I could research all the medical doctors with the initials, DJ in Jamaica. Then we'll know who this DJ is or at least narrow it down and then we call his number and see if he answers."

"Why do you want to know so badly?" Danica asked Stella. "You are making me anxious to know too."

"As you should be," Stella started stretching her arms, "no matter what you say it is not normal to be talking to someone for a year and some months and not know how they look or even how they sound on the phone. Looks are important, it gives you context and the sound of a voice too, I can bet his voice is a high soprano."

Danica laughed out loud. "I don't think so. I think it is deep, and smooth like honey."

"Good grief," Stella muttered. "Next, you'll say he writes as if he is handsome."

"I was thinking it," Danica huffed, "but it sounds too ridiculous to say out loud. I am glad you said it and not me."

"I am sure if this guy knew how you look, he would have found you already." Stella murmured. "Therefore, I am going to assume that he really doesn't want to be seen. He is desperate to stay hidden."

Danica grinned. "So you think I'm pretty, huh? You think DJ will take one look at me and swoon?"

Stella laughed. "I would be lying if I say no. You know, you remind me of Mona from the comedy Half and Half. You don't look exactly like her, your hair is lighter and wavier and your shape, superb." Stella looked her over. "I think it's your shape that will make this DJ go hmmm. I hear the young people are calling it slim-thick."

"Oh stop," Danica grinned. "Aren't you just four years older than I am, what do you mean the young people?"

"I think like an older person, I grew up with my grandparents." Stella grinned. "Anyway, we digress. You have the booty I am killing myself with squats in the gym to get. I pointed out your butt to Lee Wiley and told him that's exactly how I want mine to look, and he said it is achievable."

"You showed Lee Wiley my butt?" Danica widened her eyes. "You two stood by and admired my butt?

"Yep, you were in jeans, and sauntering past the gym, we both agreed that some women would go under the knife to have your perky posterior, and he bragged that he could sculpt my body to look the same."

Danica looked around at her butt and then giggled. "I hated it when I was younger, I thought it was too big."

"We always hate some part of us that others envy." Stella mused. "The food here is so good. If only it could go straight to my butt and not my thighs, I would be so happy. However, the women in my family gain weight firstly in the thighs and then our neck or arms never in the right places."

"The food is really good," Danica said dreamily. "I am constantly tempted by the ice cream. I wish I didn't have that to deal with. Why do they have a twenty-four hours ice cream shop opened for senior citizens?"

"Because somebody requested it, and what the residents want they get, no questions asked. You know Ace and Quade aim to please." Stella sighed. "They should restrict staff from visiting these places, and then I wouldn't have to exercise."

"They do restrict staff," Danica gave her the side-eye. "You are the one with the staff vouchers. How often do you write one for yourself?"

"Too often," Stella grinned. "As the gatekeeper to the cream I get giddy with power. Do you want a voucher for this evening?"

"No." Danica looked out at the view. "I said I was tempted, but I can't give in, if I eat ice cream my skin breaks out into welts and my face puffs up like a frog, it's not pretty."

"It's hard to imagine your skin looking crappy, it looks so perfect now," Stella said. "Like honey gold."

"That's because I now know what gives me flare-ups, and I have to keep stress to a minimum. You should have seen me as a teenager." Danica grimaced. "I looked awful. They called me floral face in high school.

"Floral Face?" Stella chuckled.

"Yes," Danica nodded, "and I wore braces. So some days I was Floral Face and other days Metal Mouth. One day I was in the store, and I overheard one of my mother's customers saying to the other, 'her mother is gorgeous, her father is good looking what happened to her, mixed children are usually pretty, does she have a skin disease or something'?"

"Really," Stella gasped. "Mixed children are not always pretty, and I can't believe some people, they have no tact or diplomacy and say things without thinking."

"I have gotten that same train of thought for most of my teenage life." Danica shrugged, "it didn't help that my parents are above average in the looks department. My mother, in particular, is swoon-worthy, and she has never had a pimple in her life. Well, not any that lingered."

"And you are an only child?" Stella asked.

"Only child. Only girl. To a woman who still gets catcalls in the street. Random strangers offer to marry her, boys come to my house just to see her, she's the one I got the shape from."

Danica swiped away from her conversation with DJ and held up a picture of her mom for Stella to see.

"Your mother is lovely," Stella said, "and young!"

"Yep," Danica nodded, "she married my dad on her eighteenth birthday, and she had me when she was nineteen."

"Some people start their families early, don't they?" Stella grimaced. "At eighteen, I was torn between going to college or start working to earn some money. I ended up doing both, I had no time for relationships, much less marriage."

"My mother's adoptive family, all married young." Danica shrugged, "it's a thing with them, my grandmother constantly bemoans the fact that I am an old maid."

Stella chuckled. "She needs to get with the times."

"Because my mother grew up with that mindset when I was at the grand old age of eighteen, she started to panic that I had never had a boyfriend or had any prospects.

"I didn't even have a date to go to my senior prom, so my mom paid one of the church elders' son to take me. It was supposed to be a secret, but he told me when we got there, and he found somebody else to his liking. I demanded a refund for my mother. The idiot gave me back the money and told me sorry, he wasn't that into me."

"Oh, honey," Stella looked at her sympathetically. "Is that why you are content to be speaking to strangers on a dating site because you can't get over your dismal teen years? Do you still think you are floral face, Danica, with no date to the prom?"

"No!" Danica gasped. "It's not that. And I looked good for the prom. I used a lot of makeup to cover up my spots. Of course, the day after that, I had breakouts on top of my unhealed breakouts because I was allergic to the make-up, but I know I looked good that night. My date just liked someone else who went to my school."

"So help me to understand," Stella folded her arms and looked at Danica, "why would a lady who looks like you, with such a pretty face and a great bod' have to resort to Christian Singles several years after high school?"

"There was an incident a couple years ago." Danica looked away from Stella. "I don't want to talk about it. Needless to say, because of that incident I stopped dating. I actually went to a therapist."

"A couple of dates in my past would send me to therapy." Stella murmured.

Danica chuckled. "My therapist said I was ready to get back into the dating world and suggested that I should join the site. There was no pressure, there were no pictures, and I would just talk to people who shared the same interests as me.

"I didn't have to meet them if I didn't want to, I could tell them as much or as little about myself as I wanted. That appealed to me."

"Ah," Stella nodded, "it is all making sense to me now. So Christian Singles is really for people who are damaged and in hiding."

"No," Danica said in exasperation. "Not everyone is

damaged or even hiding. I think this started because people couldn't find someone in their church to date, and they wanted to talk to people who had the same value system. In the dating world, it's a mixed bag. With Christian Singles, you can only be referred by someone with a verifiable affiliation to a church body, so I guess that simplifies matters somewhat. Even though I am well aware that people in the church can be as bad or even worse than people outside."

"So, this DJ person, you read his profile and instantly liked him?" Stella was skeptical, it dripped from her every word.

"Yes," Danica nodded, "basically."

"Let me see his profile," Stella said, "and I'll tell you if he is a fraud. I have the fraud sniffer right here." She pointed to her nose. "I have narrowly missed trouble because of this sniffer. It never lets me down."

"Well, his profile is not public anymore." Danica smiled. "We went private a couple months ago, when we exchanged numbers, but I saved it. I liked it. While I was scrolling through, it caught my eye. I contacted him and said hi, and we took off from there."

She held out the phone to Stella, who took the phone from her gingerly. She had her critic face on. She started reading out loud:

Hi, my name is DJ. I am a fun-loving guy who is pretty laid back. I live in the tropics, Jamaica to be exact.

My friends would probably describe me as cool and calm. My feathers are not easily ruffled. I am very big on family. Mine is tightly knit. I love children and animals. My job is pretty demanding. However, I find time for swimming, tennis, and hiking, and I dabble in music. Of all my hobbies, I find that hiking clears my mind and gives me some quiet time to put things in perspective. I love spicy foods, and I am always up for a cooking challenge. This year, I am trying to perfect some Indian recipes. If you know how to cook with garam masala. Hit me up, and we can chat.

Stella stopped reading and looked at her. "What's garam masala?"

"The English translation is hot spices." Danica grinned. "Doesn't he sound perfect?"

"Humph." Stella handed the phone back to her. "He doesn't sound too bad. What made you choose him?"

"He said he was from Jamaica; I have been coming back here since I was five. I have a little obsession with everything Jamaican. He is big on family, and he loves to hike, all his hobbies are basically my hobbies, and I adore Indian food. It felt right when I read his profile."

"I see," Stella said. "He does sound legit. I wish you had a picture though."

Danica sighed. "I guess I can't argue that out of you."

She yawned widely and then looked at Stella. "Sorry, I still feel a bit sleepy. I think I'm going to forego our obligatory lap around the field."

"Ah yes, I heard about your adventure yesterday evening with the girl who hopped a ride on the tour bus." Stella nodded. "I am sure Lily or Quade will be calling me about it this morning as soon as I sit at my desk, but unlike you, I slept like a baby last night. I think I have a lap or two left in me."

Stella headed off to the field, and Danica sat on one of the spectator benches, "I might convince myself to join you."

She glanced at her phone. She could do with one more text from DJ. She hadn't gotten a lot of rest last night after she had unwittingly picked up a passenger when she had taken her group on tour.

One of her clients, a sweet octogenarian who had lived in the hills of Trelawny, had begged her to swing by a place called Crimson Hill so she could see how the place had changed.

On their way back from Crimson Hill, they made a rest-stop at Falmouth, the capital of the parish. That must have been the place where they picked up their stowaway.

They only found out that she was on board when they arrived at Golden Acres. She had walked out of the bus with a busted lip and a cut on her forehead. The top of her clothes had been bloody from the head wound. Apparently, she had crouched down at the back of the bus and had hidden quite well behind the picnic gear.

She had shocked everyone with her presence when they had alighted the transport.

The stowaway said her name was Grace, and she was hiding from something so terrible she couldn't tell them.

It was a good thing Ace Jackson was still on call that evening. He had looked over Grace, dressed her wounds, and put her up in one of the staff accommodations. She hoped Grace would find refuge here, and this would be the beginning of a better life for her. She figured that eventually, Grace would be willing to tell her story, she just needed time.

Danica looked over at the slowly rising sun in the distance. She loved this time of the day; everything was so fresh and new.

She checked her phone for the affirmation of the day, which was faithfully sent to her every morning by her friend Miranda from college, who was now a clinical psychologist.

She read it and laughed out loud. It was so accurate.

She usually sent it off to DJ because she shared her daily affirmations with him.

Stella ran past her and panted.

"That's one lap, lazybones! What are you laughing about?"

Danica grinned. "You know what the affirmation of the

day is today?"

Stella didn't slow down to hear her. "You are going to have to catch me and tell me!"

Danica got up and ran beside her. "Today's affirmation says: I am starting over, a new pattern of thoughts, a new wave of emotions, a new connection to the world and those around me. I am now ready to accept a happy and fulfilling relationship."

Stella stopped running. "You sent that to DJ?"

"Yup." Danica nodded, "and I meant it too."

"I just hope he is not some kook," Stella muttered before she started running again.

Chapter Two

I am now ready to accept a happy and fulfilling relationship.
Deuce read the affirmation that Dani had sent him. Did she
mean it, or was this just one of those everyday ones that she
usually sent?

She had put a smiling emoji beside it and a thumbs up,
which meant it was personal, it was almost as if she was
reading his mind.

He wanted to meet Dani. It was time he met her face-
to-face, and they could finally explore something that he
thought could last.

He didn't want to be waiting around when Kelsey stepped
up her campaign for them to get back together. He wanted
a happy and fulfilling relationship this time around, and he
wouldn't get that from Kelsey. Deep down he knew that he
and Kelsey were never going to work.

They had tried so many times at having a relationship, but
it always imploded.

This time he wouldn't be the pathetic sod that Kelsey could wrap around her finger. He had Dani in his life, and he wanted to start over as that affirmation said.

Six months ago, Dani had told him she was in Jamaica. She had come at a time when he was filling in for his friend at the children's hospital, and he had no time to pursue a romantic interest, at least that is what he told himself.

That was then, and this was now. He now had time. He was back in regular practice, which meant he had time for himself, and he didn't want Kelsey on his mind.

He texted Dani, *I am going to take this one to heart, we'll talk about it later, have a nice day.*

It was time to head to work. He had a packed schedule.

The complex where he worked was pragmatically called the Medical Complex. More than fourteen doctors with different specialties had their offices there.

There was a pharmacy, a lab, and a gift shop. He shared his building with an obstetrician, Amanda 'Mandy' Mohan. They also shared a receptionist. Their building was a bright and cheerful space. Deuce loved pediatrics because he enjoyed working with little people.

Beside their building was Dr. Cleveland Parks', a dentist, his upstairs area was empty, Cleveland was actively looking for someone to split the rent with. Deuce parked beside Cleveland's Ferrari. Their designated parking space was beside each other, but it always gave Deuce a little jolt of anxiety to pull up beside the expensive car. Once Cleveland had gotten a scratch on the thing, and it had cost him an arm and a leg to fix.

"Hey man," Cleveland called to him. He was just getting out of his car too.

"Hey, Cleve," Deuce nodded, "What's up?"

"I'm getting company," Cleveland said. "Didn't you hear?

Dale Julius is going to join me here. I am going to have an orthodontist. We are a perfect fit, don't you think? Like you and Mandy."

Deuce let the news sink in. Everyone knew about his history with Kelsey and Kelsey's unexpected marriage to Dale Julius and their subsequent divorce.

Cleveland probably expected him to spontaneously combust at the news that his supposed love-rival was going to be next door.

"Dale will make an excellent addition to your practice," Deuce said, "you've always wanted a complimentary specialty, you should be happy."

He didn't prolong the conversation, though Cleve looked like he wanted to say more. He entered his building. The reception area was empty for now. Mandy was standing at the desk, peering at the schedule.

"Welcome back, handsome," She looked up. "I wish I had a welcome banner. It would say something along the lines of, *welcome back to full-time practice. Now you can sleep at night.*"

Deuce smiled. "I doubt that. I'm afraid the sleeping part might not be true. I'm going to be haunted by the ghost of Kelsey and her ex-husband. Dale is going to be next door, and Kelsey is already talking about us getting back together."

"She doesn't waste time, does she?" Mandy widened her eyes. "I never liked that girl."

Deuce sighed. Mandy was an old friend, and she knew all the drama with him and Dale and Kelsey. When Kelsey left him the last time, Mandy was the one who encouraged him to sign up for Christian Singles, because that is where she met her husband.

"I spoke to Dale this morning," Mandy said. "He came in very early. I helped him to bring in a box or two. He said he couldn't wait to erase the last few years from his mind, and he's hoping that you two can be friends again."

"I don't know about that," Deuce grunted. "I would find it a little awkward."

"Well, you two do have Toxic Kelsey in common." Mandy looked at him assessingly. "You're not planning to go back to Kelsey, are you?"

Deuce didn't answer. He couldn't predict the future. It was not the first time Kelsey and he had broken up, and he had gone back to her after one of her other relationships fizzled out.

"Don't!" Mandy said warningly. "It won't work. What does God have to do? Send an earthquake, lightning, thunder? Why don't you stop hiding behind the screen and find that girl you have been talking to on Christian Singles? Isn't she in Jamaica?"

Deuce frowned at Mandy. "Imagine you saying that. Today she sent me an affirmation about accepting a happy and fulfilling relationship, and I was thinking the same thing. I think it is time we took this to another level."

"Good!" Mandy said. "I never understood why you were so hooked on Kelsey. It's not even as if she is all that. Behind that baby doll-face and that serine smile, is a viper. God help us all now that she's back."

"I'm not going to bash Kelsey," Deuce said. "As a matter of fact, I'm not going to talk about her any at all."

By and large, Deuce kept to his word. Kelsey did send him a picture of herself with a tear in one eye and a message that said, *I'm sorry for all the things I've done*. He deleted it before he could weaken.

At the end of the day, he was in the parking lot, contemplating what he was going to do next. He had a group practice with his brothers in half an hour. And he was invited to one of his patient's, birthday party.

He would drop in and leave a present. The patient in question had beaten cancer two years running, and his parents thought he had something to do with it.

Deuce went to the gift shop. He knew exactly what to get his patient. The little boy loved puzzles. He headed to the puzzle aisle and ran into Dale Julius.

Dale Julius was the same height as he was. They had about the same complexion, and they were about the same size.

Obviously, Dale had not let the last three years of doing his fellowship, mess with his physique. But that was where their similarities ended. Dale Julius had a broader face, wider nose, and enviably straight white teeth, naturally perfect teeth. It had not been a major surprise when Dale Julius had chosen orthodontics as his specialty.

He smiled at Deuce, flashing his teeth. Deuce had been prepared for a certain coldness between them, but Dale Julius was not transmitting that vibe.

"DJ," he said warmly. "It is nice to see you."

"What's up, man?" Deuce nodded.

Dale Julius walked over to him and shook his hand, pumping it fiercely.

"I've wanted to talk to you in the past three years, but I was afraid."

Deuce frowned at him. "Why?"

"Because I married Kelsey," Dale sighed, "and we all know how you felt about Kelsey and she about you. I shouldn't have put myself in the equation. I should have waited until you two did your breakup makeup dance instead of insinuating myself in something that I had no business being in. I had no clue what I was getting myself into."

Deuce was fascinated by the outpouring of honesty. When they were in med school, Dale had never been so open with him. Dale always gave off the vibe that he was hiding something. He had a secretive personality. What you got from Dale was usually given after many months of him keeping it hidden, even if it was nothing major.

So this openness was new, and despite him saying that he didn't want to know anything about Kelsey and her relationship, he was eager to hear more from Dale.

"What do you mean?" Deuce asked Dale. "And why did the two of you break up anyway?"

"We broke up because she is crazy," Dale said. "Besides, I think she married me because she wanted you to feel jealous or something. I went along with it because I had always liked her. It was the biggest mistake of my life. It almost drove me crazy," Dale said. "We didn't even stay married for two months. We moved to Canada to do our fellowship together. You know, she did hers in Rheumatology?"

"No, I didn't," Deuce said. "I haven't been keeping tabs on her like that."

"Good for you." Dale looked around the store and looked over to the other aisle and came closer to Deuce.

"Kelsey has issues. That is all I'm going to say about that. I thought I was a good enough friend to you that when you heard that we were going to get married, you could have said something to me."

"What are you talking about?" Deuce asked.

"Kelsey is selfish, narcissistic, and obsessed with you."

"Really?" Deuce raised an eyebrow. "How obsessed could she have been? She had me but was always leaving me, and how can you be a narcissist and obsessed with a person. Shouldn't one cancel out the other?"

"It's weird," Dale said, "and maybe I am not using the right terms. After all, I am no psychiatrist, but I rue the day I ever said I do to that woman. After the fellowship, I was hoping that she would stay in Canada, I would return to Jamaica, and we would be a continent away from each other."

"Wow." Deuce shook his head. "I had no idea you had it so bad with her. I have never seen Kelsey as an obsessed narcissist."

"And you were her neighbor growing up?" Dale asked incredulously. "They say love is blind, Deuce, but you're taking this to another level. Or maybe you're the one person Kelsey has never shown her true self to."

"But you liked her," Deuce protested, "you liked her when we were in med school, didn't you?"

"Because I didn't know her," Dale said. "I thought she was outgoing and fun. I thought you were stupid for letting her go all the many times she left you. It turns out I was wrong."

Deuce cleared his throat. He didn't want to discuss this anymore. Obviously, he was speaking with a bitter ex-husband, and there were always two sides to a story. He headed to the games section of the store and picked up a jigsaw puzzle.

"Mandy said you joined Christian Singles." Dale followed him.

Deuce turned around. "Why would she tell you that?"

"Because I asked her about the dating scene around here," Dale said. "I want to join. I don't even mind the fact that they don't use profile pictures. After the sort of relationship I'm coming out of, I'm thinking that I wouldn't even mind dating an unattractive woman. She could be big and sloppy; I don't care. Anything would be an improvement on what I had with Kelsey."

"Jeez, Dale," Deuce said. "You're making me think that I dodged a bullet with Kelsey."

"You did," Dale snorted. "Being married to Kelsey should have come with a warning. And no, I am not just saying this because I want you to stay away from her; this is a genuine warning."

Deuce picked up the puzzle. "Okay. Consider me warned. I met someone on Christian Singles that I think I have chemistry with. I imagine she's a lovely person in real life. I've never met her, though."

"Hmm," Dale said. "Well, I'm going to ask Mandy to recommend me. As I said, I want to move on, and this is probably a good steppingstone."

Deuce nodded. "Well, I'll see you around, Dale."

"Yes," Dale said, "See you."

Deuce paid for the gift. His mind was racing as he went outside and headed to the car. In all his time with Kelsey, he had never thought of her as an obsessed, narcissist. And he had been her ex more often than anybody else.

Dale sounded bitter and a little unhinged if you asked him.

He went into the car, and for a brief moment, indulged himself in the Kelsey that he knew. He had met her when they were twelve years old...

Sometime in the past...

It was a typical Wednesday evening. They were just driving back from church when they saw a moving van in the driveway next door. Deuce had been sitting between his brothers, Ace and Trey. Ace was two years older and acting bossy. As usual, he had taken the window seat, though Deuce wanted that seat. He couldn't play the count-the-cars game properly if he was in the middle. Trey was on the other side of him. He would kick off a tantrum if he didn't get the window seat, and nobody wanted to go through that.

Trey at eight was spoiled rotten and knew how to get his way—*the brat.*

While Deuce was resentfully thinking these things about his brothers, his father had slowed down.

"I heard the new couple has two children," his mother was saying, "a girl Deuce's age, and another one Trey's age," his mother was saying under her breath. "I heard that the wife was a model, but now she is a caterer. Can you believe that? We're going to have a celebrity right beside us?"

"Which model?" His father asked.

"Amelia Fagan. She has graced the covers of Vogue and all these other magazines."

"Interesting," his father said, his voice sounding less than interested.

"I hope she's into gardening and flowers," his mother said wistfully. "I feel as if she and I are going to be great friends."

His father stopped the car abruptly and exclaimed, "What on earth!"

When Deuce looked through the windscreen, he saw a little girl. She was about his height, standing in the driveway glaring at them. "I could have hit her," his father mumbled, "And why's the brat glaring at us?"

"Oh, she's pretty," His mother said, "What a pretty little girl, she looks like a barbie doll. She makes me yearn for a girl."

His father had looked positively apoplectic at the suggestion, but Deuce had concurred, she did look like one of the dolls in his mother's doll collection. She had a smooth milk chocolate complexion, a cute as a button nose and deep brown doe eyes.

Kelsey had crossed her arms and was standing under the floodlights in the driveway, glaring at them. She was wearing two pigtails on either side of her head, she flicked one over her shoulders with an attitude that would be comical, if she didn't have tear streaks on her face.

They had all gotten out of the car. His father was forced to park in front of their driveway.

"Good night, little girl," his mother had said. Kelsey had looked at them all. Her look of defiance crumbling.

"I want to live over here. I don't want to live with Mommy and her new man."

"Kelsey Channer!" A cross looking lady had come out from the house that was rapidly being filled with furniture and boxes that the moving crew was bringing in. "Get over here this instant!"

"No!" Kelsey said. "I'm living with them. They seem like a nice family. Our family is not right, not without Daddy!"

And then her eyes had zeroed in on Deuce. He may have pushed out his scrawny chest a little. She smiled, her red lips turning up in a bow.

"I'm going to be your friend," She had declared.

It had been the beginning of their friendship; he had convinced her to leave their driveway by promising that she could come and play with him in the daytime.

Kelsey had been a handful for her mother and stepfather. She was a daddy's girl and blamed her mother for the divorce from her beloved daddy. She never got on well with her stepfather, their quarrels were legendary. Everyone knew Kelsey as the girl who would shout, 'you are not my father, you can't tell me what to do,' at the top of her voice in the neighborhood.

The poor man could do no right in Kelsey's eyes, and she hated living with them. She had been the same with her father's new wife too when she had demanded to go and live with her dad, and her father had sent her back to her mom. She had been too disruptive in that household too and her parents were at their wits end to pacify her heartbreak.

One day when she was about fourteen, Deuce found

Kelsey sobbing on his veranda. She had probably slept there too. She had taken to sleeping on his veranda just so that she could worry her mother and have her assume that she had run away.

She had looked at him, her eyes red and swollen. "I have no one, I belong nowhere. I hate them all. I only have you, DJ."

****

He had been protective of her ever since, and even now, after hearing Dale's scathing review of Kelsey, he was feeling sympathetic to her. Maybe if he didn't know her back story and her turbulent years of feeling rejected, he wouldn't feel as if he needed to be the only stable influence in her life.

But he was moving on, wasn't he? His history with Kelsey didn't matter anymore.

Chapter Three

Danica entered her modest-sized office inside the admin building. The sign read- Recreation Department with a little man hiking with a backpack.

She smiled when she saw it. It always gave her a special buzz to come upstairs. They were at the far end of the admin offices, so she had to pass, Quade Jackson's offices. He was the chief operating officer of the place, but he also ran an extensive real estate empire. He had made Golden Acres his operation base because he liked the view.

He had two secretaries and an assistant.

His assistant Devin Johnson passed her in the corridor and gave her a shy smile. Danica could not remember Devin looking her in the face. He was always nervous around her. Stella had speculated that he could be the DJ she was writing to, but Danica had rejected that assertion. Devin didn't seem like the type.

But who was a lying type though?

Danica argued with herself. She just didn't get a DJ vibe from him. Besides, DJ was a doctor.

She waved and smiled at Devin, who reddened around the ears. Definitely not DJ. Danica chuckled to herself. She imagined that DJ was confident and quite at ease with women. He certainly wrote that way.

She passed Quade's suite of offices and then Lily Pikeman's office. Lily was the administrator at Golden Acres. She was the one who ran things. She had an imposing presence, and so the staff was a little afraid of her.

Beside Lily's office were HR and Accounts. Stella was already at her desk and on the phone. She had an open-door policy; Danica could see inside her office.

Danica waved, and Stella waved back. The stowaway girl, Grace, was sitting in front of Stella's desk. Someone had found her clothes that fit, and she was all cleaned up.

She turned and looked at Danica.

Danica slowed down and gawped. The woman was beautiful, despite the bandage over her head. She had mocha colored skin and long kinky hair plaited in two thick ropes that covered a bandage at her neck. Danica had not seen that cut last night. Obviously, Grace had more injures than Danica had thought.

"Is everything okay?" Danica walked closer to the office and whispered.

Grace nodded. "I am waiting for Stella. Dr. Ace told her to find me a job."

"Good." Danica nodded. "I wish you the best."

Grace smiled at her tentatively. "Thank you for saving my life."

"It was no problem at all," Danica smiled. In truth, she hadn't done anything except drive to Crimson Hill at MaryBeth's request.

"Maybe one day, you will save my life too," she said to Grace jokingly and winked.

Stella came off the phone, Grace turned around, and Danica continued on to her office.

She had a brief meeting with her team, and they had some adjustments to make to the schedule. There were four of them in the department, and Phyllis had called in sick. Now they were down to three, and they had sports day planned for the end of the week in collaboration with the fitness and nutrition department.

It was the worst time to be a man down, especially that the 'man' in question was Phyllis, the energy bunny.

Her staff was already there: Opal and Tony. They were drinking coffee and reading the day's newspaper.

Opal looked up. "Hey boss lady. What are the real deets on the trip to Trelawny? Tony said you guys picked up someone."

Danica nodded. "We did."

"So, it is true." Opal widened her eyes. "I was thinking that Tony was pulling my leg. Why doesn't anything exciting happen when I come along on one of these tours?"

Danica chuckled. Opal was an outgoing girl in her early twenties. She was a hilarious one-woman entertainment act who had the residents always requesting that she come along on the tours.

In fact, she had put on solo shows for the residents on theater nights. They preferred Opal to many professionals, which suited Opal quite fine. She was paid separately for her entertainment gigs.

Phyllis was off sick, but when she is well, she was also high octane. Tony of the four of them was more laid back and a great listener. She usually assigned him to be in charge of the more relaxing pursuits.

She was the newest one on the team. She knew she had big shoes to fill, both Opal and Phyllis waxed poetic about Amelia, the previous recreation director.

Amelia near qualified for sainthood when they were done.

Opal even had a picture of the group on her desk, and she looked at it fondly, especially when Danica was handing out the rosters for the week.

She always said a prayer before she met with them, especially Opal. They made her anxious to succeed. When she worked in her parents' sporting goods store, she had never been under this type of pressure.

She glanced at the affirmation that she had framed and put above the conference table. It was definitely her meeting mantra.

Start comparing yourself to yourself, and no one else. Forget what others have and where they are. You are not walking in their shoes, and you'll never comfortably walk in your own if you keep comparing yourself to them.

She inhaled and then exhaled. It was a source of pride to her that they couldn't tell from her demeanor that she was somewhat rattled. It was only a matter of time before she stopped comparing herself to Amelia.

"So Phyllis is off for the rest of the week," Danica said, "that means we are going to have to divvy up her work."

She handed them the week's schedule.

"Please, please don't give me Mrs. Julius." Opal said, looking it over. "Phyllis was supposed to meet her this morning to discuss the start of a reading club. Mrs. Julius and I have a clash of personalities, she thinks I am not deferent enough to her. I had to go and look up the word deferent."

"It means polite submission and respect," Tony smirked.

"So you know words," Opal glared at him, "let him go and kiss Mrs. Julius' toes. She accosted me in the lobby to complain about our lack of books in the library. I may or may not have been grumpy that morning, and I told her that most people now read from their devices. She took that to mean that I had no deference."

"I can't do it," Tony looked at Danica, "though I would want to, I love to read. I have an art exhibit to set up in the lobby. Dorothy and the gang would crucify me if I don't show up."

"Dorothy and the gang," Opal chuckled, "they have him wrapped around their little finger, and he likes it."

"As he should," Danica smiled at Tony. "Don't worry about it, I'll do it. A reading club is actually a great thing to add to our activity list, and I'll look into the library. Where is it again?"

"The poky room beside the arts and craft center, it doesn't even have a sign on the door," Opal said. "Amelia didn't think it was our responsibility to direct people to read. They either liked it or not."

"Well, I am not Amelia," Danica said, "and reading is an excellent activity to encourage with seniors. It improves memory, enhances imagination, helps with depression, and exercises the brain. It was a lovely suggestion from Mrs. Julius. I am thinking of a reading competition, quizzes with prizes…"

"Oh," Opal said, getting into the spirit. "Maybe even have a book drive to stock the library, some of these people have lots and lots of books sitting around."

Danica nodded. "That's an excellent idea. I'll suggest it to Mrs. Julius. Maybe that is why she was asking about the library."

"Could be," Opal said chastened. "But she is just so snooty and has this way of looking down her nose at you, it rubs me the wrong way."

"Everybody rubs you the wrong way," Tony muttered.

They discussed the schedule and chose what they wanted to take over from Phyllis and then went about their day.

Danica had the meeting with Mrs. Julius at ten o'clock.

She decided to do some research on starting a reading club. It wouldn't hurt to find out as much as she could so that she could offer something sensible to the conversation.

She looked up Mrs. Julius' profile on the Golden Acres database.

She was in Bungalow four, just two doors down from Danica's grandaunt, Florence Jackson.

Leona Julius, age 67, widowed, three children, no grandchildren. Her hobbies were reading and painting.

Her former profession was financial analyst.

At precisely ten o'clock, she knocked on Mrs. Julius' door. Each bungalow was separated by privacy trees and a small lawn. It was beautiful, but the real beauty was at the back of the bungalows. They had a view of the city below and the sea in the distance. All the bungalows had patios to take advantage of the view.

Leona opened the door a crack.

"I am Danica Hunt. I am here about the reading club, I am filling in for Phyllis today, she is not well," Danica said in as friendly a voice as she could manage.

The door opened a bit more, and Leona stood there. She was a tall, dark woman that looked nothing like sixty. Maybe early fifties. Her picture on the Golden Acres site did her no justice. She looked like she could be related to Sheryl Lee Ralph, the mother in the sitcom Moesha. Danica was still watching reruns of the comedy.

While Danica was processing all of this, Leona Julius was staring at her too, a frown on her face, waiting for Danica to continue. She automatically smiled when she thought about that.

"Can I come in?" Danica asked, "or would a later date be acceptable to you?"

"Do you read?" Leona asked haughtily, "I have no time to be discussing a reading club with people who do not read. Phyllis was reading a particular book I wanted to borrow, hence the idea of a reading club."

"I see." Danica nodded. "I do read. I love it, actually."

"Name your last book." Leona crossed her arms and looked at her suspiciously.

"Er…" Danica bit her lip and then remembered the bodice ripper she had found in her aunt Florence's library. She had liked the title.

"Dishonorable Intentions', I don't remember the name of the author. It was a historical romance about this servant whose Duke had died on their way to the colonies, and he took the Duke's place and married this wealthy heiress, she had never met him so she was none the wiser about who he was originally."

"Intriguing." Leona grinned and opened the door wider. "Come on in."

The bungalow was the same light and airy space as all the other bungalows on the property. All of the dwellings were single-story accommodations. Mrs. Julius had a hammock on her patio.

"I love lying out here, not at nights," Mrs. Julius said. "It does get a little chilly."

She headed to the patio and sat in one of the comfy-looking chairs. She indicated for Danica to sit before her.

"Tell me more about the story."

"Well, they threw the real duke overboard and…"

"No, don't say another word," Mrs. Julius held up a finger, "you have to lend it to me."

"I can ask my aunt, Florence Jackson," Danica said, "I doubt she would say no."

"You are a pretty girl." Mrs. Julius said, changing the subject. "Are you married?"

"No," Danica smiled. She wasn't offended, all the older people she came into contact with at Golden Acres usually asked her the same question. It was par for the course.

"All my children have disappointed me in the marriage department," Mrs. Julius said ruefully. "It is my fault, of course."

Danica listened politely. She had come to realize that older people sometimes just needed a listening ear.

"I left them with my husband's parents to work in Cayman when they were young. My husband had just died, and I had to go back into the working world. I was a housewife who had never used her business degree. I had no one to leave them with at the time. All my relatives live overseas.

"I had no idea that the Julius' were not the best parents. My husband was normal, and they seemed nice when we visited, but goodness, they weren't."

"What did they do?" Danica asked.

"They were abusive. By the time I realized that my children were living with monsters, it was too late. All my children were messed up. I spent many years trying to make up for that mistake, and now that I am retired, I am putting my all into developing relationships with them."

"I am particularly proud of my youngest. I know all mothers say that their son is the best, but my youngest son is the absolute best. He is a compassionate man; the earlier years don't seem to have affected him as much as his older siblings. He is the one I am closest to, and I would do anything for that boy. I just want to see him happy."

Danica smiled, hoping that Mrs. Julius would move on to

the reading club, she looked like somebody who was settling in for a long counseling session about her regrets in life.

There was a full-time psychiatrist on staff. Danica was wondering how she could suggest visiting him when Leona got up. "I just had a thought."

"Huh?" Danica looked at Leona confused.

"You are single, and my son is single. Isn't this amazing? He's a doctor, you know," Leona said proudly. An orthodontist, to be exact."

Danica smiled. She sounded proud enough to burst.

"Such a pity you have perfect teeth," Mrs. Julius said ruefully, "or else you could take a visit to see him."

"I should have perfect teeth, I was wearing braces since I was eight, I only stopped wearing retainers when I was twenty." Danica grimaced, "Mrs. Julius, I should clarify that I'm not exactly single. I have been talking to someone for a while, though I have never met him, I think our relationship is on the path..."

"I think I'll go with the first answer," Mrs. Julius interjected. "You said you were single, and I'm sticking with that. Wait, hold it right there. I have got to show you a picture of my baby. You'll like him, he's handsome like his father."

She went to her living room and came back with a stack of photographs. "Tada, here he is. Here is my Dale."

On the top of the stack, there was a graduation picture, someone had scribbled the words, *Dr. D. J.*

Danica suppressed a gasp.

Could this be DJ?

The DJ that she has been speaking to for a year and some months.

This was him?

He was handsome as his mother had bragged, he had two deep dimples when he smiled.

"Your son could be Lamman Rucker's twin."

"Lamman Rucker?" Leona frowned. "Will Brown in Meet The Brown's?"

"That's right." Danica nodded and looked down at Dale Julius' picture again.

"There is a likeness, but my Dale is better looking," Leona said jovially. "He's good looking, isn't he? "

Danica's mind was racing. So, this could be DJ. He was really a doctor.

She looked up at Mrs. Julius, who was looking at her knowingly.

Danica stuttered. She could barely get the question out; her tongue was tripping over itself. "Has he...has he... ever mentioned a dating site called Christian Singles?"

"As a matter of fact, he has, but there is no need for that. You are right here. He is here. Well, not here at Golden Acres, but he is in the same parish. You two should meet in the old-fashioned way. He said he doesn't need me to be setting up a date for him, which is quite ridiculous. I have an instinct about these things, and I have a feeling you two would get on like a house on fire. Especially after his little situation with Kelsey."

She laughed and sat down beside Danica.

Her perfume washed over Danica like a cloud.

Danica's eyes widened. Was Kelsey the K that had broken his heart. She looked at the picture again. She couldn't believe it.

She had found her DJ. In the most unexpected and weird way.

"I have a good feeling about you, Danica." Leona patted her arm.

"You have to promise to come to dinner at the end of the week when Dale visits. He is going to spend the weekend with me."

"I promise," Danica said huskily and then cleared her throat. "Can we discuss the reading club now?"

"Of course, dear." Leona said, "Dale loves to read too, you know."

Chapter Four

Deuce had a busy day and only got a chance to check his phone just before going to bed. He saw a message from Dani.

Do you know Leona Julius?

Yes, he typed back.

I met her today! Dani responded. *She is an interesting woman.*

Deuce closed his eyes. He was too tired to ask her where she had met Leona and what had they talked about, all the kind of things he would be asking her if he wasn't so tired.

Leona Julius certainly was an interesting woman, Deuce thought tiredly, she had moved from housewife to financial tzar in no time. There was an urban legend that she had been so fierce she used to eat her competition for breakfast.

He remembered reading an article about her before he and Dale became friends, and he had been quite impressed with her business persona. Unfortunately, all of that was at the expense of her children. She barely had a relationship with any of them now.

Dale had called her funding his med school education guilt money.

Dale had confided in him one night when they were pulling an all-nighter in the library. It was the week before Mother's Day, and Deuce had been going on and on about his gift for his mom, a vanilla orchid. He was still marveling about the fact that vanilla beans came from orchids.

And Dale had been listening with a faintly bored air.

"Do you know what I am giving my mother for Mother's Day?" Dale had looked at him blearily.

"No, you never said," Deuce said. "You don't talk about her much, do you. I heard they wanted her to head up the central bank here. I was waiting for you to say something."

Dale snorted. "I don't care. I hate her."

Deuce had looked at him, his mouth hanging open. "Hate is a strong word for one's mother."

"I shouldn't say hate, I should settle for mildly dislike. I hated her a couple of years ago, it is mellowing out now." Dale grimaced, "and I am getting her nothing this year because she doesn't deserve it. My college tuition is guilt money. The clothes she buys me, and my monthly stipend are hush money payments."

"Why?" Deuce had asked.

"That woman left us with the worst people on the entire island," Dale said, "and she knew they were bad, and she did nothing about it and she could have, she eventually had to find us different guardians when they died."

"They couldn't be that bad," Deuce said. "There are murderers and pedophiles…"

"My grandparents were murderers and pedophiles," Dale said simply, "and if they hadn't died in a car accident, one of us would have killed them. I am thinking Candice, my big sister, she was the most bitter, the most abused. She is the one who had to sleep with the old man."

"What?" Deuce had looked at his friend in alarm.

"And he made us watch too," Dale said, "the louder she screamed, the more he liked it. The more disgusted we looked, the more he enjoyed it. We couldn't escape the room either because he would lock the door, lock us all in."

Dale had looked back down at his book, and Deuce had looked at him a disturbed feeling running up his spine.

"You must have told someone."

"Yes, I did." Dale sighed, "my mother. She told me to bear it out for a month, she would send for us. However, she got a promotion, and they sent her to Canada, and the month turned into a year. So she asked us to wait a while longer. She said her move was good for us, she said that she would make more money and we would all benefit. She was building a better life.

"And then Candice got pregnant for the grandfather and lost the baby, and Brad tried to commit suicide and then the grandparents died in a car accident.

"The car brakes failed," Dale said it with such pleasure that Deuce had been afraid to ask if he had anything to do with it.

Deuce had tried to forget what he had heard about Leona Julius through the years, but the first time he had met her at Dale's graduation, she had shown up acting all motherly and proud, he couldn't hide his dislike for her.

Leona had sensed it. She knew that he knew, and she had given him a wide berth.

Deuce still disliked her on behalf of Dale even though he was no longer Dale's friend. He didn't know how any of the children, especially Candice, coped after what they went through.

Leona had been an accessory to a terrible crime against her children.

The trip down memory lane had drained him. He closed his eyes. It had been a busy day, and all he wanted to do now was sleep.

A ping indicated that another message had come in, and he reluctantly checked his phone. It was Malik Holt from Sunrise Medical. *NEED A CONSULT. Call me tomorrow as early as you can.*

Malik was the resident pediatric surgeon at Sunrise Medical. Deuce had worked with Malik several times. He usually had no problems hopping over to Sunrise Medical to discuss or even to perform a surgery with Malik, but this time he was reluctant.

Sunrise Medical was Kelsey's backyard, and he didn't want a run-in with her. However, he knew it may be unavoidable.

When Malik wrote in all caps, it usually meant that the situation was urgent. He tried not to think about Kelsey, but like earlier today, when Dale Julius had mentioned that she was an obsessive narcissist, little patches about their past kept coming up to him.

Kelsey may seem obsessed with him, but the truth was, he knew what really happened in her early years, he had a front-row seat to her turmoil when her parents had married other people, and she had felt abandoned.

And twelve-year-old Deuce had vowed to always be there for her. Her safe haven. And she tested the boundaries of their relationship every time because she knew she could.

Maybe that's why a little part of him was afraid to engage with Kelsey again. He feared that he would succumb to her just because she was Kelsey.

He closed his eyes tiredly. He wasn't going to lend himself to one more thought about Kelsey or Dale.

He thought about Dani instead. Not for the first time, he envisioned what she looked like. She had described herself as multiracial and moderately attractive.

What was moderately attractive?

He fell asleep thinking about it.

****

Sunrise Medical was a buzz of activity when Deuce drove up Tuesday afternoon. Malik Holt wanted an opinion on a surgery he had to do. It was supposed to be a fifteen-minute visit, and then he would meet Trey in the cafeteria for lunch. He rarely met with his little brother these days, and he was looking forward to it.

However, Malik's case turned out to be a little more involved than he thought, and Trey was waiting for him with his finger on his watch.

"I have surgery in ten minutes," Trey said, "but I know you gotta eat, so I'm just going to follow you to the cafeteria. You know we have a five-star chef on staff?"

Deuce grinned. "If Sunrise Medical knew how much you promoted them, they would appoint you to head of surgery."

Trey threw back his head and laughed. "I am a mere resident, brother dear. Don't tell me we haven't seen each other for so long, you think I finished training."

A few of the ladies in the cafeteria turned to look at them.

Everyone smiled.

His brother was quite popular with the women at Sunrise Medical.

Deuce shook his head. "Are they still calling you the playboy doctor?"

Trey grinned. "Not since I started quoting scriptures at them. I have been memorizing whole chunks of the Bible lately, their eyes usually glaze over when I start off my statements by saying, it is written."

Deuce chuckled. "Have you seen Kelsey lately?"

"Mostly every day," Trey said. "She did her fellowship in rheumatology, you know." Trey grimaced. "And she's walking around here with an attitude that says, look at me, lowly resident scums, I have a special specialty."

"So, same Kelsey, then?" Deuce said.

"Nah." Trey shook his head. "She cut her hair and dyed it blonde, and she has a small tattoo that reads *Dr. K*, with a stethoscope around it. She said it was a divorce present to herself."

Deuce snorted. "Enough about her. What's going on with you? We haven't been able to hold you down for practice in four weeks."

"I know," Trey said. "I am beat. I don't set my own schedule like you, Ace and Dad. I'm at the whim of my assigned schedule. I am only a resident."

"For just another year, and then you are done." Deuce smiled at him. "I am proud of you."

"Thanks, man," Trey nodded. "You know I actually love general surgery, who would have thunk it? Little old Trey from rehab to surgical table, it's a god comeback story."

"I always knew you had it in you." Deuce patted him on the back.

They picked up their food and headed to a small table that overlooked a lovely courtyard.

"So, what's new?" Trey grinned. "You still talking to that girl on Christian Singles?"

"Yup." Deuce nodded.

"I should join." Trey made a face. "Next year, when I finish my residency and get my life back. Things are so bad now I have no time to dwell over the fact that I am celibate.

I thought it would have been hard, but I am strangely too stressed to care." His pager went off, and he looked down at it and groaned. "I'm going to have to run. I have someone's bladder to remove and then sew back together."

Deuce made a face. "Sounds like routine stuff."

Trey laughed. He picked up a bread roll and then stood up. "I'll have to walk with this to my office. Love you bro, but I've gotta go."

Deuce nodded. "Someone should put that on a t-shirt."

Trey laughed.

Deuce was just getting into his lunch, enjoying the succulent chicken breast and roasted vegetables, and occasionally glanced at the courtyard. He didn't know what alerted him to her presence.

He was deep in thought and couldn't remember what he was thinking. Kelsey stood over him with a tray in her hands. "Earth to DJ."

Deuce looked at her. "Hmm."

That was all he couldn't manage. He was taking her all in at once. She was in the requisite white coat. She had cut her hair and dyed it blonde, as Trey had said.

The style fit her, emphasizing her sharp cheekbones. Her eyes looked a little tired around the rims and red as if she was crying or rubbing them. That was something else about Kelsey that he had forgotten. She acted like nothing bothered her in general, but she could cry at the drop of a hat, especially if she saw someone else crying.

"Is this seat taken?" she asked while sitting down anyway.

"How are ya, DJ?" She waggled her thick, shapely eyebrows at him. "I knew you were here. I heard the nurses in the lobby talking about a tall, dark, handsome doctor who looked like the model Ryan Gentles without the locks, and I knew they were talking about you. I always told you that you looked like him with a little less beefcake, but still…you have always been genetically blessed."

"You just licked your lips when you said that," Deuce said mockingly. "It's okay to greet me without the flattery."

"It's not flattery. Have you seen yourself in the mirror lately? I haven't seen you in three years, and it looks like you have gotten better looking."

"Which just goes to show even good-looking guys get kicked to the curb and rejected just like everyone else." Deuce gave her a half-smile. "So, how have you been?"

"Quite good," Kelsey said, "now that I've seen you. Seeing you made my day, DJ."

"I can't say the same, Kelsey."

"I knew you'd say that," Kelsey sighed. "You don't respond to my texts. I was beginning to get desperate, but here you are, like an answer to prayers."

"You pray these days? Deuce asked skeptically.

"I see I'll have to do some groveling," Kelsey smirked. "And yes, I do pray."

"Groveling won't work," Deuce said.

"I am sure it will. I just need to give you time to remember how it was." Kelsey inhaled. "I'm happy to see you today. I've always wanted to say this face to face. I was wrong…"

"I've heard this before," Deuce snorted. "I wish I could eat in peace."

"No, you haven't heard this, DJ, trust me," Kelsey said solemnly, her face downcast. "I have never admitted that I was wrong. I have never humbled myself before. This time, DJ, I'm going to do whatever it takes. You are the best thing that ever happened to me, and I foolishly let our relationship go."

"We were drifting apart anyway," Deuce stared at her stonily.

"That's true," Kelsey said, "we were both knee-deep in our career, and we hardly spoke to each other. I was spending more time with Dale than I was with you, and he really poured on the romance, flowers, and chocolate and attention. To be frank, I thought you and I were over."

"We were over." Deuce sighed. "And I am not sure why we are having this conversation."

"I made a big mistake with Dale. He has issues, like two different personalities, a raging maniac and a crying baby. Complimentary in public, emotionally abusive in private. The six months married to him was six months too long."

Deuce frowned. "Funnily enough, I saw him yesterday, and he said the same thing about you. He said you have issues. He called you an obsessed narcissist, so I'm not sure who to believe."

"Believe me," Kelsey said. "He is the obsessed narcissist. Behind that affable smile and that calm manner is a crazy human being. He knew you and I were drifting apart, and he really worked himself into my space. I fell for it; I am ashamed to say. I am one of those women who took the sweet-talking and the flowers and chocolate shtick and fell for it." Kelsey sighed.

"It didn't take a week into our marriage for me to realize that I made a mistake. The mask fell off so fast, the idiot groomed me, reeled me in, made me think that he was awesome, but trust me when I tell you living with him was no joke. He made me doubt my own sanity and sense of reality.

"Not to mention his constant put-downs and comparing me to other women and claiming it was a joke when I called him out on it. And he insisted on me dressing a certain way and wearing my hair a certain way and…"

Kelsey paused and looked at Deuce. "The final phase was

the bullying and intimidation. I couldn't do it anymore. I was tired of getting up and feeling worthless, so I packed my stuff and left. If he calls me an obsessed narcissist, he is passive-aggressive, and he wanted to control me."

Deuce cleared his throat. "You sounded like you had a tough time."

"And then some," Kelsey laughed dryly. "Dale wanted someone to dominate as if somehow that would make him a man. He is damaged from whatever trauma happened to him in his childhood. You could have told me about his messed up past you know, he has never sought help for it. If I had known about any of that and the fact that he hadn't addressed it, I wouldn't have married him. I bet you were happy to see me making a huge mistake."

Deuce sighed. "I don't wish ill for you, Kelsey. I never have, and I never will."

"You are a thousand times better than that man," Kelsey said. " I heard he's working at the Medical Complex where you're working. Keep him at a distance. Don't let him know what you're about. I'm warning you, DJ. He's crazy."

Deuce sighed. "Why didn't you stay in Canada? I could do without the drama."

"If I could have taken this weather there, I would." Kelsey smiled, showing her perfect teeth. Her smile lit up her face, coercing him to smile with her, but he didn't feel like smiling.

"And besides, you were here. I want to make one last-ditch effort to let you know how awful I feel and how sorry I am, DJ. I will always love you, and only you."

"There was a time," Deuce drummed his fingers on the table, "when this speech would have made me happy, but there is someone else."

Kelsey slumped her shoulders. "I should have expected it. You're handsome, wealthy, and have a nice personality. You tick all the boxes. Only an idiot would have let you go, and I have since acknowledged that I am a big one. Who is the lucky girl?"

"Nobody, you know," Deuce said abruptly.

"I hope she knows what she's got."

Deuce didn't respond. That was the thing. She had no clue who he was, and he had no clue who she was. That was something that needed to be changed as soon as possible.

Chapter Five

After his conversation with Kelsey, Deuce was more than certain that he wanted to meet Dani. It was time, he was already feeling a weakening towards Kelsey, a certain sympathy. He couldn't have that. That was how it always started.

He didn't even make it to the car. He texted Dani and said, *I've been thinking about your affirmation, I think it's time we meet.*

It wasn't long after that she sent a text, saying - *This weekend?*

Deuce almost texted back— *What about today? What about right now?* but he changed his mind. Maybe this weekend would be better for her, but it seemed so far away, and he had a niggling feeling that this weekend was going to be too late.

He stamped down that over-the-top emotion, and instead asked her- *where?*

I'll think of something, gotta go, she texted back.
Staff meeting

Deuce smiled with himself. He was finally going to meet Dani.

He always wondered what the Dani stood for. Was it Danielle? Was it Dania? Was it just an alias like his name?

There was no use speculating, he would find out this weekend. Though they were close to meeting, he couldn't help but wonder how she looked.

He was only human, after all. She had described herself as having brown hair, brown eyes, and olive-toned skin. He had often wondered if something was wrong with her physically. She had not pushed to meet him, and he had been quite okay with that. He liked her caution, it meant she wasn't particularly desperate.

Besides, it didn't matter if she was pretty or not, he wasn't hung up on beauty.

Kelsey was beautiful and look where that got him. As a matter of fact, that had been the appeal of the Christian Singles dating site.

It was a place to put in your description, without a profile image attached. There was no need to lie about looks by using a stock image, and there was no need to admire someone and then be sorely disappointed when you saw them in person.

Deuce got in the car and drummed his fingers on the steering wheel. *This was ridiculous.* He had only known this girl through text messages, but he had felt an affinity to her just by her written word. He even remembered the words of her profile. He had remembered thinking that she was creative and funny.

He thought about it and smiled. She had written- *Hi, my name is Dani, I am relatively uncomplicated. I like raindrops on roses and whiskers on kittens, bright earth tone colors and anything written, I like hiking and tennis and playing on swings, these are a few of my favorite things.*

She had him humming the song, *My Favorite Things,* when he thought of her.

That's why he had started talking to her after looking at many profiles. She had further stated that her idea of a date was to go hiking somewhere scenic, and she loved to travel to out of the way, non-touristy places.

He had liked that about her. Not that he had done much traveling lately.

They had options for their first date. They could go hiking, he was looking forward to that. Holywell was a scenic area that he had never gone to with a girl.

Deuce looked at his face in the mirror. At least she wouldn't run away screaming when she saw him. Females tend to do the opposite, and he wasn't arrogant when he said that; his friends thought it incredulous that he was using a dating site.

He drove to work with a little fissure of excitement zinging through him.

He was looking forward to this weekend, more than he thought he would have been. Maybe it was that meeting with Kelsey. Maybe it was the fact that he knew that he needed to move on, and it made no sense for him to delay this inevitable meeting with Dani.

When he stepped into the waiting area, he saw that Dale Julius was talking to his receptionist. "There you are," Dale said. "I was just asking Mia if I could make an appointment."

"What is it, a consult?" Deuce asked.

"Unfortunately, it's not business-related," Dale grinned.

Deuce frowned at him. This guy was going to be a nuisance; he could feel it. He figured Dale was trying to overcompensate, trying to push a friendship where there was none for a while now.

"You don't have an appointment until forty minutes," Mia said to him, not helping the situation. "Your last patient canceled."

Deuce nodded. "Very well. Come along, Dale. We will have a personal conversation."

Dale followed him to his office. He sat down and looked around.

"I like your decoration," Dale said.

"I'm a pediatrician," Deuce looked at him. "My decor is supposed to appeal to children. The mural on that wall was actually painted by a patient of mine."

"I like kittens and clouds. Maybe it's the kid in me," Dale grinned. "I can't tell you how excited I am to be working right beside you."

Deuce made a face. "Really now?"

"Remember when we were in college? You were Batman, and I was your faithful sidekick, Robin."

"You were around me a lot," Deuce said. "Faithful sidekick, I don't know about that."

"I almost did my residency in pediatrics, you know." Dale chuckled. "I always wanted to be you."

"I can't see why," Deuce said. "I was no one special."

"But you were." Dale leaned back in his chair and folded his arms. "You came from a loving family, and your mom was always so accommodative and sweet. I envied your relationship with her and your siblings. I thought you had the picture-perfect life. I also liked the fact that you had a girlfriend that you loved to distraction. Maybe that's why I married her in the first place. I wanted what you had."

"Where are you going with this?" Deuce asked.

"I am just saying," Dale said, "I hope there are no hard feelings because I married your ex-girlfriend, and I'd like us to be friends again. I'm serious about it."

Deuce didn't want to respond, one way or the other. He didn't want to be friends with Dale again.

There was something about Dale that got on his nerves, and it had nothing to do with the fact that he married Kelsey or that Kelsey had said that he was two-faced.

Deuce couldn't shake the feeling that any friendship between them would be inequitable. Dale had never been a true friend; he was more a sycophant who thought that he could buy friendships with his mother's money.

He had tolerated Dale because he knew of Dale's family background. That night in the library, when Dale had confessed how messed up his childhood was, had actually been a turning point in their relationship.

It had gone a long way into explaining why Dale was so attached to him and interested in his family. It was because he had none.

Before he had found out Dale's history, he had thought that Dale had liked him a little bit too much, so much so that Deuce thought had he had been gay.

The more he had tried to get some distance from Dale, the more Dale had forced himself closer. It was almost stalkerish, the way he would show up in various places in the past. That side of his personality had always made Deuce uneasy. He didn't want to be ensnared like that with Dale Julius again.

He since realized that Dale was just needy. It was sad that he hadn't taken advantage of the therapy his mother had paid for. Dale had skipped most of the sessions in college, and he still hadn't sought help to deal with his childhood trauma.

"Anyway," Dale was speaking again. Deuce missed half of what he said, "my mother is living at Golden Acres, she took out a long-term lease."

"Oh, she is?" Deuce raised an eyebrow.

"She loves it there," Dale said. "She said it's like living on a cruise ship without being at sea."

"So, you two have buried the hatchet?" Deuce asked. "The last time I heard you speak about her, you snarled when you said her name."

"We agreed to put the past behind us," Dale murmured. "She is trying hard to be in our lives again, and I am trying to meet her half-way."

"I even promised to spend my weekends with her until I can find a more permanent living situation, I have been staying at a vacation rental. I am searching for a permanent base."

"How are your brother and sister? Deuce asked. "Have they forgiven her?"

"She speaks to Brad once a year at Christmas. I call him, and he grudgingly tells her hello when she insists."

Deuce nodded. "What is he doing with himself now?"

"He is a technical writer; he writes auto mechanics textbooks," Dale said proudly. "He lives in Texas; I don't know where specifically because he doesn't tell me specifics. He is afraid I will tell our mother."

"That's sad." Deuce murmured, but after hearing how the crash happened, he was wondering if the grandparent's accident had been an accident after all.

"My sister is changed though, she has forgiven all and moved on." Dale was still talking. "She just doesn't want to have anything much to do with the past. She has gotten very religious and not in the mainstream kind of way..." Dale sighed, "she speaks like the original King James Version of the Bible, and she changed her name to something Hebrew."

Deuce chuckled. "Really?"

"Yup," Dale nodded, "she speaketh in verilies and thuses. I can't understand her half the time. My mother says she cannot sleep after talking to Candice. Candice takes pleasure in telling her about all the stories of children being abused and the kind of things they go through and how she rescues them. I guess I am her only living relative who is making an effort."

"That's admirable of you for forgiving your mother and forging a relationship with her." Deuce looked at Dale. "Unless, of course, you are just hanging on for her money."

"She owes me, she is the reason why I am the way I am." Dale growled, "I was emotionally and physically abused as a child, she knew it and did nothing until it was too late."

"You should get help with that, Dale," Deuce said gently, "you have unresolved childhood issues. They will manifest themselves in your everyday life."

He didn't want to add and your personality and how you respond to situations. Dale looked like he was barely hanging on to his emotions. He went from calm to riled up in a few moments.

"Enough about that," Dale wrangled his emotions back under control and was once again talking to him in a friendly way. "How soon after joining this Christian Singles dating site did you meet the person you have been talking with?"

"Ah," Deuce nodded, "so that is why you're here."

"Guilty!" Dale grinned. "I have been curious ever since Mandy told me about Christian Singles. I found it odd that there were no profile images, but I can work with that. So how soon after talking on the app, did you meet the girl you've been talking to?"

"I haven't met her yet," Deuce said. "We've been talking for a year and a half, about six months in we went private and started texting each other exclusively. It was just today, I decided that I wanted to meet her, and she said she's ready, so we're going to meet this weekend.

"She's the only one I've talked to. I mean, there is no

other Christian Single that I've talked to, so I really have no experience to offer."

"That's okay." Dale narrowed his eyes. "How did you know she was the one you wanted to speak to?"

"Her profile sounded fun and creative," Deuce said. "She likes a lot of the things that I like. She has a wicked sense of humor, and that comes out in her texts. I just like her, and I just wanted a simple, uncomplicated relationship at the time."

"Hmm," Dale said. "So, you use your initials or pen name or real name?"

"I use DJ," Deuce was getting impatient with the conversation.

"So how do you keep up with your conversations and all of that?" Dale asked.

"I have a stellar memory," Deuce said, "and besides, I save all of our text messages. I haven't deleted one." He looked at his phone. "You know, I was thinking that one day if we actually got together, I would print them, and I could use it as an anniversary present or something."

"That's a great idea!" Dale said, "I didn't know you were so romantic, DJ. Maybe you could give it to her when you meet this weekend. That would be a gift you guys could share."

"That's not a bad idea," Deuce said, "but I am biding my time. I think it's a momentous gift, and I might not like her after I meet her in person."

"Ah," Dale nodded. "I never thought of that. You have never seen her, so you don't know if you and her will have face-to-face chemistry, do you? It's interesting."

"Part of it is also the anticipation of seeing her for the first time. I can hardly wait."

"I can imagine," Dale said. "I want to anticipate too. I am

joining it."

Deuce frowned. He didn't think it was wise for any unsuspecting woman to be in Dale's sphere. He needed to work on his past issues before he dealt with anyone else. He wondered if he should say anything about Kelsey's conversation.

It bothered him how she had accused him of not letting her know what kind of background Dale was coming from.

He hadn't thought about it at the time. Besides, she wouldn't have listened, Dale was the one who God had ordained for her she had said. He remembered the snarky little text she had sent him.

He cleared his throat. "Dale, maybe you should see a therapist before you start seeing anyone."

Dale laughed. "You have been talking to Kelsey, my creative ex-wife. Did she say I whipped her at dawn and made her walk barefoot in the snow?"

"No." Dale raised a brow. "She said you were emotionally abusive. Maybe you are manifesting traits from your past and not aware of it."

"She was the one who was emotionally abusive, and trust me, I lived through it. I can recognize it a mile off." Dale snorted. "It was so bad, if I never see or speak to her again, I'll be fine with that."

"It was nice having this chat," Dale said. "Maybe we can have lunch now and again."

Deuce shrugged non-committaly. "Maybe."

****

"You are not going to believe this," Danica said before she sat down. The staff cafeteria was almost empty. Only Danica, Stella, and Lee Wiley, the hunky fitness instructor, were there. Stella was staring at him and drooling. She forked the food into her mouth slowly while she watched Lee Wiley. To his credit, Lee was finding her attention quite amusing.

Danica snapped her fingers in front of Stella's face. "Earth to Stella."

"He is so fine," Stella said. "It's not the muscles. It's the eyes. Do you realize that he has those eyes? Those piercing eyes?"

"Ace has it." Danica chuckled. "I don't see you staring at him like you can't move."

"I used to," Stella made a face. "I had a crush on Ace, his brother Deuce, and Trey and I had a crush on my boss, Quade. It all passed for every single one of them, but this thing for Lee Wiley is sticking."

"Maybe because you two work in the same space?" Danica said. "You know, funny enough, I've never met Ace's brothers. I have been here for six months, and I've never met one of them."

"You are missing out," Stella said. "Deuce is yummy times two, and Trey is scrumptious times three."

Danica laughed. "Anyway, I have something to tell you. I think I've found DJ. I know who he is, and I found that out on the very day that he says he wants us to meet."

"Say that again," Stella said.

"I found him," Danica said excitedly. "I know who he is. His name is Dale Julius, and get this, his mother has a bungalow here."

"Ah," Stella said, "The plot thickens."

"And she doesn't know that I know that he is the DJ from Christian Singles. She mentioned that he joined Christian Singles, and she finds the whole online dating thing ridiculous. She wants me to come to dinner with her and her son."

Stella widened their eyes. "Say what!"

"And the funny part about all of this is that DJ is asking if we can meet, and I said this weekend. He doesn't know what is going to hit him."

"Amazing," Stella said. "Did you see a picture of him at his mother's place?"

"Oh, yes," Danica nodded, "and nothing is wrong with him, as you've been implying. He is tall, dark, and handsome."

"Well, there are days when the skeptics are proven wrong," Stella said. "I'm happy that this is working out for you, and he's not a short baldy who is trying to hoodwink you into thinking he is something he is not."

"He's not a short baldy," Danica said, "and looks should not matter."

"Keep telling yourself that," Stella looked pass Danica and on Lee Wiley again.

Chapter Six

Dale Julius entered the grounds of Golden Acres and looked around the landscape with satisfaction. His mother had chosen well. He had to admit that he had been skeptical when she first told him about moving to a retirement home in Jamaica. He didn't know if he wanted to live with her so close to him, that was the reason he had left Canada in the first place, to put some distance between them. But this could work out. Leona Julius was morphing into the person he had wanted her to be in his childhood, at least she was making an effort.

He parked before Bungalow Three, as his mother had instructed. She was standing at the door with a broad smile on her face.

"Dale, my beautiful baby boy. I wish you could visit me every day."

Dale kissed her on her cheeks. "You know, I was getting acquainted with the new practice and all."

"I know," Leona smile at him sweetly. "How is that going?"

"Doctor Cleveland is accommodative, but the rent at the complex is not cheap."

"I'll pay for it," Leona said without batting an eyelash. "I've been telling the ladies in my little group at the recreation center that my son is now an orthodontist."

"Mom, you brag too much," Dale said. "Show me inside, let me see what you have going here."

"It's wonderful here," Leona said. "They have different layers of security, the food is good, the people up here are friendly... I guess most of us came here so that we can have friends and companionship. I am even going to start a reading club and stock the library here. I was talking to the head of the recreation department, an absolute sweetie pie. She came by to discuss the new venture with me, and I learned that she's single."

Dale rolled his eyes. "Mom."

"You need to move on from Kelsey." His mother looked at him, reprovingly. "I told you, you shouldn't have married that girl. Now you have a divorce beside your name. My son, the divorcee."

Dale looked around while his mother rambled on. This conversation was nothing new. "And to think, you have to resort to online dating."

Dale headed to the patio, and his mother followed. "Well, I found the girl for you."

"I'm not interested, Mom," Dale said. "Can you show me around?"

"Sure," His mother glared at him, "but I'm sure you'll be interested when you see this girl."

"Describe her," Dale said.

"She's a good-looking girl who seems very sweet." Leona frowned. "But best of all, she is single."

"Interesting," Dale said flatly.

"We're going on a trip." Leona ignored his tone. "She frequently takes the residents on tours all over the island. I think it gives her as much pleasure as it does the residents. I've never been on one of them, as you know. I'm new here, but they'll be going to Negril soon, and I'll be going with them."

"Good for you," Dale said. "It sounds like absolute fun up here."

"Oh, it is," Leona shook her head. She showed him around the three-bedroom bungalow, gushing over all the amenities. "This is money well spent. I am considering making this a long-term investment. Let me show you around the compound."

His mother was talkative, and Dale was soaking it all in. They headed to the recreation center. The place had a spectacular view of the city below and even beyond. Dale started walking behind just so he could see the view. Leona patiently waited for him in the reception area.

"It's really nice," Dale said.

"Upstairs," Leona indicated to the winding staircase, "is where they have the administrative offices, downstairs is where we have recreation, gym, restaurants, all of that jazz. There's a lovely restaurant here called the Chocolat'. It would make a perfect place for your date with Danica."

"You still going on about Danica?" Dale asked. "I don't need any help, you know, Mom."

"You might not," Leona said, "but she does. You know she was on that ridiculous online dating app like you...Christian Singles."

"She was?" Dale widened his eyes. "You sure?"

"And there she is," Leona whispered, "the golden girl."

Dale whistled involuntarily.

She was gorgeous, she had satin-smooth skin, plump red lips, and a perfectly proportioned shape with a little extra on her hips. She had her hair in a high top not. He stood there, and he could literally imagine himself kissing her neck.

What were the odds that this Danica girl was on Christian Singles? Deuce Jackson was on Christian Single. He had to find out what Deuce's girl's screen name was. Danica was in deep conversation with Quade Jackson. He seemed as if he headed into what was a suite of offices, and she followed. He watched as her shapely derriere disappeared.

"You're sure she was on Christian Singles?" he asked his mother, faintly. Seeing the girl made him lightheaded.

Leona cackled. "Told you, you would like her."

He had to find out if this was Deuce Jackson's text pal. *What had Deuce said, he had never met her?*

Dale chuckled to himself, this was the perfect opportunity to beat Deuce Jackson at something because he saw her first.

****

Deuce couldn't find his phone after lunch. He walked into the office to find Ace waiting for him.

"Trying to call you," Ace said.

"I can't find my phone." Deuce was in a panic. "I looked everywhere. Do you know what this means? I can't text Dani."

Ace looked at him incredulously. "You can't find your phone, and that is what you're worried about?"

"I have to set up a meet with her this weekend." Deuce shook his head. "This is so weird."

"Sorry about that, Bro," Ace said. "I hope you find it soon."

"Me too," Deuce said. "There is probably no need to panic. So how's it going? Dr. Jackson. How is Kiya? You two still in the nauseatingly lovey-dovey stage, aren't you?"

Ace laughed. "No need to sound so jealous."

"I am not jealous," Deuce said. "I was going to be in the lovey-dovey stage soon, with my mysterious text pal, Dani. But now, I can't find my phone."

"I actually thought that Kelsey would have gotten through to you," Ace said, "and that you would have forgotten about your text pal by now."

"Nope." Deuce walked toward his office, and Ace walked behind him. "If anything, seeing Kelsey recently strengthened my resolve to move on. And the best person to do it with is someone I've been talking to for the past year. You know, I've known her longer than you've known Kiya."

Ace grinned. "Okay, but do you guys hang out every night, cook together, laugh together, play games together, have physical contact?"

"No to all of the above." Deuce looked at his brother, balefully. "Sounds like you two are having fun."

"Except last week." Ace rolled his eyes. "Her ex-boyfriend, who is currently married to her sister, was in town. He went to her business place to beg her to come back to him. I was just in time to pick up Kiya for lunch, and she introduced us."

"And no doubt you puffed out your chest and beat it with your fist and said, 'she's mine, she's mine." Deuce laughed.

"Actually, no," Ace said. "I was quite polite. I knew he was married to Kiya's sister, and Kiya had moved on, and so I enquired after his wife. He got the message or at least I hope he did.

"You know what would send an even bigger message?" Deuce said. "Marry her."

"I'm working on that," Ace said, "I do not have the luxury of a year and a half, like you and your mysterious text pal.

It's been just two months since we met. We're still getting to know each other."

Deuce chuckled. "Ah, so that bit about knowing my text pal longer than you know Kiya struck a nerve with you, didn't it?"

"Speaking of exes," Ace ignored him "I hope you don't mind, but Quade wants to ask Kelsey to come and work with us on a biweekly basis. We have many cases that she could help us with. She's a rheumatologist after all."

Deuce shrug. "I don't care."

"You're sure," Ace raised an eyebrow.

"Very sure," Deuce said. "I just need to get back my phone."

"Retrace your steps," Ace said. "When did you notice it missing."

"I couldn't find it when I got home yesterday evening." Deuce drummed his fingers on the table. "I was talking to Dad in the parking lot when Dale came over, sucking up as usual... He always used to say he wished Dad was his father."

"You guys are friends again?" Ace widened his eyes.

"He's trying to get back in my good graces," Deuce shrugged. "I can't blame him for marrying Kelsey. We were finished at the time."

Ace wrinkled his brow. "You were finished, but still... I remember how it was when you heard that Kelsey got married. You were devastated, and you were doubly devastated when you found out it was to Dale Julius."

"And now I'm not devastated or care much," Deuce said, "besides his office is next to mine."

Ace grimaced. "Well then, isn't this all modern? It sounds so all-in-the-tribe, especially if you and Kelsey end up together again. Kelsey would have married your friend first, and then you. I'm sure you would invite Dale to the wedding, wouldn't you?"

"For the love of..." Deuce shook his head. "I'm not marrying Kelsey! I'm hoping to have something going with Dani."

Obviously, Ace did not believe a word Deuce was saying. He changed the subject.

"So what happened after you spoke to Dad and Dale in the parking lot?"

"I excused myself and went into the office for something. When I got back, Dad and Dale were gone, and I drove home, and there was no phone. It could be that it fell out in the parking lot between me going to the office and back. I'm not sure."

Ace looked at his watch and got up. "I hope you find it soon. I sense that you'll need it. You have a lot riding on this Dani girl who you've never met, don't you?"

"Will you stop saying I've never met her? I know her, and I know stuff about her. We know each other. Having a relationship face-to-face is overrated," Deuce said.

Ace laughed. "Oh, yes, overrated."

"Get outta here," Deuce said good-naturedly.

Chapter Seven

Deuce had to get a new phone. It was the day after his phone went missing, a Wednesday, and he still had not contacted Dani. The weekend loomed before him. He didn't even know if it was lost or not, but he was still holding out hope that it wasn't.

"Are you going to join us for the surgery at Sunrise Medical," Mandy asked. "I know you consulted with Malik about it."

"I did consult with him," Deuce said. "but I forgot to call him to confirm that I will be there. Maybe he called me, but I do not have my phone."

"He called the office," Mandy said, "Just a gentle reminder for you to be there. At least there is one positive to this…" Mandy paused dramatically.

"What?" Deuce asked.

"Kelsey won't be calling you anymore, not until you find the phone."

"And my problem is," Deuce sighed, "neither will Dani."

Unsurprisingly, he was feeling a sense of loss about the whole situation. He was near panic now. In the past year and a half since he and Dani have been talking, he had spoken to her every day. He looked forward to her daily affirmations.

He was feeling a little bereft at the absence. He logged into Christian Singles, but it was fruitless doing so; they had privatized their profiles. Hers would not be up. His searching was futile.

He remembered the day they had decided to go private; they had basically confided their secrets to each other. She had confided in him the harrowing reason why she didn't date. She had gone out with a guy from her church, and he had attempted to rape her after she refused to invite him up to her apartment after a third date. Apparently, three dates in the guy's eyes meant it was time to get intimate.

Her neighbor had been walking his dog when the guy had held her down. Dani had said it was divine intervention because no one would usually be on her street at that time.

She had serious trust issues with dates in enclosed spaces.

And he had confided in her that every time Kelsey left him for someone else, it had chipped away at his self-esteem. Of course, he didn't say Kelsey he had said K, but the point was that he had never shared that with anyone else. He seemed okay on the outside, but he was slowly degenerating.

It had felt liberating to admit it to someone. He didn't have those kinds of soul to soul declarations to anyone, and he marveled that it felt right saying it to Dani.

That was the very day he started taking things seriously with her, and he had made his profile private.

He thought he would have no more need for Christian Singles, but now he wished that they were still public because he had not memorized her number. She had recently changed her phone to a local service provider when she came to Jamaica.

It weighed on his mind all day and way into the night.

He was standing in the courtyard after the surgery. He was bone-tired, but the surgery had been a success.

It was a little after three in the morning, and a little boy now had a better chance at life. Kelsey joined him in the courtyard.

"You look bright-eyed and ready to face the day," she joked.

I might look that way, but my personal life is bust, Deuce thought darkly. "What are you doing here at this hour?" he asked her.

"I never left," Kelsey chuckled. "There was an emergency with one of my patients, but it's all sorted now. Besides, I live nearby. You want to come over and see where?"

Deuce contemplated Kelsey, looking at her feature by feature until she started to squirm. "We had great sex, didn't we?" Deuce asked out loud.

Kelsey nodded eagerly. "The best. Do you remember that time after we finished Human Structure and Function finals, and it was raining, and you didn't bother to go to your place? Both of us were a little jaded after that exam, and we both swore up and down that we had no energy for anything else, but when we got to my place..."

Deuce closed his eyes. "I remember, Kelsey, It's memories like that kept me up at night whenever you broke up with me."

Kelsey sighed. "We only broke up three times, DJ. It was not that many. I wouldn't call our little fights, and then make up a permanent thing."

"So which are the big three in your eyes?" Deuce asked.

"The night you first asked me to marry you." Kelsey looked

pain. "We were just twenty-one, and it was Valentine's Day."

"I remember it clearly," Deuce nodded. "I thought I was going to get the resounding yes. We had been so close."

"But I wasn't ready for all of that," Kelsey said. "Back then, I wondered what if the grass is greener elsewhere, what if I could find more excitement? We had only ever been with each other."

"And there was nothing wrong with that," Deuce snorted. "You broke my heart, trampled it, squeezed it up, and threw it to the dogs."

"I know," Kelsey said, "but it didn't hurt as much the second and third time, did it? In essence, I did you a favor the first time."

"Some favor that was," Deuce snorted. "You broke my heart then, and you broke it every time we broke up, the wounds were always fresh, and they hurt. I don't know. I think the worst pain was three years ago when I heard you were marrying Dale. You used to make fun of Dale.

"You called him my shadow, a lousy imitation, and yet you married him. I could never understand why?

"Sometimes I think about it and wonder why Kelsey would marry Dale. Of all the people in the world, Kelsey married Dale Julius.

"Was it to punish me? Was it to rub it in my face? I proposed so many times, and you turned me down, but you married him the first opportunity you got. I don't know if I was brokenhearted or my ego just felt as if it was trampled on."

Kelsey swallowed and shoved her hand in her jeans pocket. "The last time we broke up, the third time, it was because I felt there was a void in my life. I felt like I needed to fill it with something different. I reasoned that you were too stable and settled, and every time I came back to you, it's because I panicked. So I said this time I'm not going to panic."

Deuce snorted. "Ah, female reasoning."

"I asked myself," Kelsey continued, "what if I could find more excitement? Then I found out that Dale Julius was going to Canada on the same fellowship program as I was. I thought at the time that it would be a wonderful adventure to go overseas, to be away from you so that we wouldn't get back together. Dale had seemed different at the time. He had felt different. His personality had changed from med school, or so I thought. He was romance and adventure wrapped up in one."

"And I wasn't romantic or adventurous?" Deuce asked.

"I didn't say that," Kelsey said. "You were familiar and stable, and a little piece of me thought that meant boring. I was stupid for thinking that. Relationships are not always about fireworks and colorful displays. I would die for familiar and stable now."

"That's quite mature of you to admit that," Deuce chuckled. "I would never associate Dale with fireworks and colorful displays though."

"Oh, he knows how to charm." Kelsey sighed. "Too bad, he never managed to keep it up."

"He must have been some charmer, you married Dale the first month of being in Canada." Deuce raised his eyebrows. "The one thing I kept asking you for was commitment, but you decided that Dale would make a better husband?"

Kelsey sighed. "I was an idiot. He only decided to marry me because I turned you down, and he has always, low-key, wanted to be you."

"Rubbish," Deuce muttered without heat.

"When we first had sex? It was as if you were there with us." Kelsey made a face. "'Did DJ do it this way, what did he say, how did he react?' It was creepy." Kelsey shuddered.

"And it never got better."

Deuce looked at her in shock.

"The point is," Kelsey said, "I am different. All of this has taught me a lesson. I'm ready to commit to you and only you."

Deuce wiped his hand across his face. "Don't you think it's too early in the morning to be having these kinds of speeches and soul searching?"

"I think it is the best time to do it," Kelsey said. "Sometimes, I wake up at this time, and I meditate and ask God for guidance, but my thoughts always come back to you."

Deuce half closes his eyes and looked at her. "And you know, I meditate too. And God is telling me to stay far, far, far away from you..."

"Is that really God?" Kelsey asked, "or is it your ego?"

"I have someone else," Deuce said, "and frankly, I want to give that relationship a chance. I have a certainty that she and I can work, and I don't want to let it go. I don't want to be with you again, Kelsey."

"I respect that," Kelsey said, "but sometimes our destinies are forever entwined."

"And sometimes we tell ourselves that," Deuce said, "but it could be all a bunch of rubbish. I'm going home. Good night... morning, Kelsey."

Chapter Eight

It was Friday night. Danica was staring at the three yellow outfits that she had placed on the bed as if they would speak to her. She was spending the weekend with her aunt Florence; whose bungalow was two doors over from Leona Julius'.

She paced the room anxiously. The nights in the mountains were chilly, so she chose a sweater-dress with long bell sleeves.

Her aunt stuck her head through the door. "Aren't you going to get ready? What time is dinner?"

"Seven o'clock," Danica said. "and it's just two doors over. I have half an hour to go."

"You look pretty," Florence smiled. "I hardly ever see you in makeup, you look glamorous."

"Thank you, Aunt Florence, I finally found natural makeup that doesn't break me out. Maybe I'll glam up more often."

Florence leaned on the doorway. "You know I can't imagine you as a floral face kid being mocked and teased and hiding out in the corner."

"That's because I finally came into my own." Danica chuckled. "My mom used to say, 'Danica, you will grow this out, you wait and see.' I guess my mommy was right."

Florence cleared her throat. "Er... Danica. Suppose you don't like this DJ fellow. I mean, there is a very real possibility that he's good looking, and he writes nice texts or whatever, but what if there is no chemistry."

"But there is," Danica said. "You don't understand, Aunty. It's not as if I need to see DJ to know."

"Well, okay," Florence said skeptically. She then chuckled. "You know, through all of this texting with this DJ person, I've been speculating that it was my nephew, Deuce, Ace's brother. Have you ever met him?"

"No," Danica said.

"Such a pity," Florence shook her head. "I think you two would have made a beautiful couple, but I never said anything, and I'm happy I didn't, because see, DJ meant Dale Julius. And here you are, half in love with him already. I wish you all the best on this momentous meeting."

"Thank you, Aunt Florence," Danica grinned. Her phone rang, and she picked it up. It was Elsa.

Florence moved from the door. "Tell her, hello."

Danica did, and Elsa squealed in her ear happily. "Girl, we need to get all caught up! First off, I can't believe the rate at which things are happening around, I went away for the honeymoon, and the next thing I know Ace is a Wiley, and you are going to meet DJ tonight."

"Who told you?" Danica smiled at her cousin's happiness. It was contagious. Hearing Elsa's voice put her in a relaxed mood.

Giselle said you texted her about it." Elsa chuckled. "It took you two long enough to meet. I was on the verge of saying something. Do you know how many times I had to keep my mouth shut when I saw you or DJ?"

"So you know, Dale Julius?" Danica asked excitedly. "It's a small world. I shouldn't be surprised."

"Dale Julius?" Elsa paused. "You wouldn't believe it; I was thinking of another DJ. I could swear up and down that your DJ was Deuce Jackson. Oh my goodness. I was so wrong," Elsa sounded so deflated. "It's just that he does online dating too, but I can't remember if it was on Christian Singles."

"Aunt Florence just mentioned him too," Danica chuckled. "What a coincidence."

"Well, I don't want to keep you from your date," Elsa murmured. "I feel a little letdown. There I was on a high and now…no you and DJ."

Danica laughed. "You do sound crushed."

"I just spoke to Giselle, and she brought me up to date with what's going on in the family. Mason and I are hosting our first dinner party as newlyweds, and you are invited. It's next week Sunday at three, make sure you come."

"Okay," Danica said, "I have to go now."

"Have fun." Elsa hung up the phone, and Danica stared at it reflectively.

Deuce Jackson. She had heard about him, of course. She knew that Ace had brothers, Ace, Deuce, Trey, and Quade was the cousin.

The whole one, two, three, four naming had not escaped her, and Stella went on and on about Ace, Deuce, and Trey and how good looking they were. She sat on the edge of the bed. Why was the name Deuce Jackson suddenly ricocheting in her head?

She had ruled him out as 'the' DJ eons ago when she found out that he was in a relationship.

It didn't matter, now did it. She was going to finally meet the DJ that she was supposed to.

****

Danica showed up at Leona's bungalow promptly at seven. She knocked on the door, and after a few moments, it was opened by a tall, dark guy who looked a bit more mature than he did in the pictures his mother had of him.

She cataloged his features quickly. He had deep-set eyes, the color of molasses, dark brown skin, full pink lips, and perfect teeth. He looked much better in person than he did in the pictures, and that said a lot. He was a good-looking man. She would have given him a second glance if she saw him walking by.

He was staring at her too, his eyes lingered a bit too long at her bust, and then he smiled at her, flashing his dimples.

She smiled back uncertainly. There was something a little unsettling about the way he had just devoured her with his eyes.

"Hi, DJ," Her voice was husky from nervousness.

"Hi, Danica. Come on in. My mom is playing bingo at the recreation center, so it's just us. We can get a chance to talk face to face."

Danica stumbled a bit when she heard that. She wasn't too eager to be alone with this stranger, his mother had said it would be a dinner with the three of them, but surely, she had nothing to worry about.

This was DJ, her DJ, the DJ she had been writing to all year. Why was it that she thought it would have been different? Why was she feeling so uncomfortable about this?

Something wasn't right, something was off.

She reasoned that she was overreacting. After all, he was

a doctor, an orthodontist, he wasn't an ax murder, she knew his mother, her aunt was just two doors over.

Besides, this was the guy that she had told all her little secrets. She'd told him how lonely she had been growing up. She had told him about her bad skin and teeth and how she was bullied.

She had told him how her date almost turned into a rape situation because the guy she had gone out with couldn't take no for an answer. If God hadn't sent someone to rescue her, she would have been a statistic.

She had told this guy, standing in front of her, all the little nitty-gritty secrets that she had told no one else, but he felt like an absolute stranger.

She suppressed a sigh and stepped through the door. *What was he thinking?*

He stood in the middle of the living room, gawping at her as if he was just as uncomfortable as she was.

"So, er, Danica, would you like us to sit on the patio?" He asked when the silence stretched between them. "Are you terribly hungry? We sent to the restaurant for food."

"No, I'm not hungry," Danica said, "but sitting on the patio would be nice. It's nice this time of night."

"That's right." He smiled. "Your grand aunt is Florence Jackson; you stay at her place sometimes."

They sat in comfortable chairs on the patio. He sat across from her with his back to the view.

"Tell me," he said, "are you related to Ace Jackson and his brothers?"

"No," Danica shook her head. "My mother was adopted, as I've told you before, and didn't know who her biological family was. Then we found our grandmother. I was searching for her for ages and then we found Aunt Florence. Ace and his brothers are related to Aunt Florence by marriage."

"Oh, yes," he nodded. "I remember that." He was saying it as if he didn't remember.

"But I didn't tell you that when Giselle..."

"As in Giselle Pryce, the four-hundred-meter runner?" He smiled.

"Yes," Danica nodded, "Giselle Pryce, the athlete. She came to the University I was attending, and we met quite coincidentally. I was going to participate in a debate, and I think she was coming from her classes. She looked so much like my mom; it was uncanny. Because my mother was adopted and didn't know anything about her family, I was excited to meet Giselle."

Dale nodded. "I can imagine."

"So, after being in touch for a while, my mom met Giselle's aunt, Sharla. They took a DNA test and found out they are sisters. After that, I met my cousins, Guy, Jordan, Case, and then I found out that Aunt Florence was related to my grandmother, who we all thought had died."

"Wow," Dale leaned forward. "That's some story. Somebody should write a book about it."

Dania laughed.

She was slowly relaxing in his company, which was a relief because this wasn't an instant attraction situation at all.

"I never imagined you would be an orthodontist." She smiled. "Somehow, I thought you would be a cardiologist or something."

Dale laughed. "And I never imagined that you would be so pretty. This is actually amazing, us meeting like this. Are all the men around you blind?"

It was a smarmy question and not one that she thought DJ should be asking. He knew why she wanted to use the dating app. She started to get uncomfortable again. He was reminding her of the jerk, Greg Rafferty, who had tried to rape her three years ago. He had said something along those same lines.

She couldn't shake the feeling that she was not attracted to Dale Julius. In fact, she felt a little repulsed. She had at least expected to like him. She had expected them to have plenty of things to talk about, but he looked stumped for conversation, and she was not going to help him out.

Something was not right about this whole scenario. She needed a rescue, and she needed one badly, and then her phone rang. She hadn't been so relieved to hear the tinkling sounds of Vivaldi Four Seasons before; it sprang her to life.

It was her mother, her dear, dear mother.

She spoke to her parents every Friday night without fail, but she had forgotten to tell them that she had a date. She jumped up and stepped away from Dale.

"Hi, mom."

"You sound weird," Her mother said without beating around the bush.

"Rescue me," Danica whispered in the phone. She looked back to see if DJ had heard her. It seemed as if he didn't. His eyes were fixed firmly on her butt.

"How should I rescue you?" Her mother asked with alarm.

"Tell Aunt Florence to come and get me," Danica said. She wondered if she was whispering a bit too loud.

"Where are you?" Her mother started whispering too.

"Just do it, Mom." She hung up the phone before her mother could prolong the conversation.

"That was my mom," she said brightly.

Dale looked at her. "How is she?"

"You know she's not doing too well," Danica said and looked at him keenly. In many of their correspondence, she had told DJ that she and her mom were close and that her mother was still in her early forties and that sometimes they felt like sisters.

So when his response was, "Ah, so she's elderly and sickly."

Danica became increasingly concerned.

"Bedridden," Danica said, castigating herself for telling a lie but doing it anyway. "And desperate for attention. My poor dad is having a hard time putting up with her demands. I'll have to help him to calm her down," Danica sighed dramatically. "I'd prefer to do it at a place where I can't be heard."

"Oh," he said, "does that mean that you're leaving already?"

"It can't be helped," Danica said. "A daughter's place is with her ailing mother."

"I understand." He nodded eagerly. "We can always pick this up at another time."

"Not on your life," Danica whispered under her breath.

At the same time, there was a thud on the door. "That must be Aunt Florence," Danica picked up her purse. "My dad probably sent her to get me."

He walked her to the door and looked at her. "So when am I going to see you again, Danica? I wish you didn't have to go."

"I know, but duty calls. You must understand, you seem close to your mom," Danica said, not even pretending that she was anything but happy to leave.

He opened the door, and Danica looked at her grandaunt in relief.

"Your mother said…"

"I know," Danica nodded, "I think she is acting up again."

Florence looked at Dale. "Well, sorry about this, young man."

Dale nodded and watched her walk away. Danica could

feel his eyes boring into her back.

Florence didn't speak until they were back into her bungalow.

"Was it that bad?" Florence looked at Danica in concern. "Your mother was frantic. She said you were being held against your will."

"Worse," Danica bemoaned, "I felted nothing, and I think he's a fraud. I had told him that my mother was bedridden, and he didn't bat an eyelash. He either, A, has never read any of my texts, or B, has a serious memory issue. I don't like him, and I never want him to text me again."

Chapter Nine

Dale cowered guiltily under his mother's glare. It was breakfast time, and she had prepared quite a spread, but she would not allow him to eat in peace. "So let me get this straight," Leona said. "You spoke to her a couple of minutes."

"Yes," Dale said, slicing through the stack of pancakes that was dripping with the blueberry compote that his mother had prepared, "and then she said that her ailing mother needed to speak to her?"

"That's about right." Dale's voice sounded garbled as he chewed.

"It was a decoy," Leona said. "Couldn't you see that?"

He had thought as much. Dale swallowed. "I wonder what I said that tipped her off that I was not the right DJ?"

He wasn't stupid. From the moment Danica had set eyes on him, she had sensed that he wasn't the real DJ, and his acting skills had not chipped in. He had been warring with himself, should he act like Deuce Jackson or be himself. The internal war had made him come across as awkward. That and the fact that he hadn't gotten a chance to run through her text messages to DJ because he couldn't open the phone, he needed a password.

He had been flying blind.

"Who is the right DJ?" Leona asked, she was obviously confused. "What are you talking about?"

"I heard about her before I met her." Dale sighed. "She is Deuce Jackson's Christian Singles text pal. She thought I was him and that she was meeting him for the first time. I always lose to Deuce Jackson. He has always had a better life than me. He was born into the right family, he is loved by all who meet him, and had the best girls chasing him. I married his stupid ex-girlfriend, thinking that because she left him, she was unique. Deuce Jackson never had to watch his grandfather abuse his sister when she was just thirteen."

"So, you tried to steal his identity?" Leona frowned at him. "What are you doing, Dale? And when are you going to stop bringing up that whole sordid business?"

"When I forget," Dale said. "I can't seem to forget it. I can't easily gloss over the past; it is a part of me."

Leona sighed. "What are you going to do about Danica? You need to make this right. I engineered this very nice date for you, and you blew it, not Deuce Jackson."

"You are right, I blew it. I really liked her though, the tension between us was raging hot. She is gorgeous, and I want her." Dale grimaced "I wonder why she ran."

"So why don't you ask her and vow never to do it again," Leona asked.

Dale shook his head. "I would have to knock on her aunt's door, I am not in the mood for her to slam it in my face or hear another excuse."

"She walks in the morning by the hiking trail," Leona said,

"the trail near the admin office. If you don't dilly dally too much, you might find her coming back." Leona looked at him sternly. "Go and make it right."

Dale took an extra bite of his pancakes and then got up.

"All right, I'm going to make it right." He didn't know how he was going to do that, but he knew it did not involve him confessing that he wasn't the DJ she thought she was corresponding with. Maybe he could plead amnesia? Would she buy it? She looked like the kind of person to laugh at any spurious excuses.

Dale let himself out of the house. The morning was still foggy. It was chilly but manageable.

What would the real DJ do?

He walked towards the trail and thought hard about his past with Deuce Jackson.

He had known Deuce for years, since high school, and had tried to emulate him for more times than he could count.

His science teacher had called him Deuce's shadow.

One girl had starkly referred to him as a low budget Deuce Jackson. That had hurt. He had no doubt that if Danica met Deuce in person, it would have gone well. Deuce had always had that effect on women.

Dale had stood by while girlfriend after girlfriend had suggested that he be more like Deuce Jackson because he came on too strong. He pushed his hand in his pants pocket.

He was a man in his thirties, so this was ridiculous. He had no idea he would find himself pretending to be Deuce Jackson again. He had done it before, and it hadn't gone well.

The first time was shortly after meeting Deuce in high school. He clearly remembered the day. It was shortly after his grandparents had died. The principal had announced it in the auditorium, and he had suddenly been the focus of every bleeding heart at the school.

Deuce had spoken to him, told him how sorry he was. Out of all the expressed sympathy, he had treasured Deuce's the most because he had long admired Deuce.

He was cool, the kind of a boy who, even at fifteen years old, had seemed as if he had it all together.

From the moment he met the super confident Deuce, he had fantasized that he was Deuce. He had told one of the newest arrivals at the school, a girl he had more than a passing crush on that he was Deuce Jackson.

The girl had called him Deuce for weeks until one day he was having lunch in the cafeteria and she had spectacularly and loudly called him an imposter.

"He is not Deuce; he is a poor imitation," One girl had said. He never forgot it.

And the second time he tried to imitate Deuce; he had married the woman Deuce loved. He gave it a go for a couple of weeks, marveling at the fact that Kelsey could not see that he was playing a part.

When he had started acting like himself again, she broke it off.

He couldn't let history repeat itself. He had a chance to make Danica fall for him before she met Deuce. When she met Deuce, it was going to be over for him.

"Hey." He saw her appear out of the mist, almost in front of the admin building. He wondered if his voice was casual enough.

He could see that quizzical, untrusting look in her eyes. He was desperate to wipe it from her face.

"How is your mom?" he asked.

"Great," Danica said. "Never been better."

He cleared his throat. "Look, I'm sorry about last night. I realize it must seem strange after texting someone for so long the expectations can be a bit high, and disappointing if they are not who you built them up to be in your head. I was thinking that we could give this another shot. We just need to get to know each other."

"Listen, DJ," Danica said. "Full disclosure here because I do not want to waste any more time. It was fun talking to you… I mean, texting you for a couple of months. I'm not gonna lie, you were good company, and I did lose myself for a little and thought that it would have been something more, but I'm not feeling this."

She gave him a smile that didn't reach her eyes. "I told you about my incident with the guy three years ago. Before the 'incident' happened, I had a premonition that I needed to escape. I have listened to that voice ever since."

Dale was puzzled. *What incident?* He had no idea what she was talking about.

She narrowed her gaze and looked at him. "Well, I'm feeling the same way now. I won't text you again, and it would be my pleasure if you don't text me either. As a matter of fact, I would love it if you would just lose my number."

She walked away, leaving him puzzled.

He gritted his teeth. He wasn't going to give up, he would just have to find a way to work around her issues. She had no idea that he didn't do very well with goodbyes.

Chapter Ten

Monday was a drudge for Deuce. He was battling the onset of the flu virus that he was sure he had gotten from one of his little patients. From the moment she had sneezed into his face, he had known he was going to be fighting the flu. He had taken all the usual precautions, high doses of vitamin C, etcetera, but he knew there was a war going on inside his body. He felt a little lethargic and had a low throbbing headache.

He had finally given up on his phone. Trey had been on his case to sync his Google contacts with that phone, but he hadn't. How he wished he had listened to his brother. He would have Dani's number now, but it was gone. Why couldn't it have been his work phone that was lost? That phone was synced, his contacts preserved.

He stopped at the phone company and reported the phone lost and got back his number by the time he left. However, he had lost the contacts that was lost in the ethers.

He wondered how Dani spent her weekend, and how she was handling him not responding to her texts. Did she think he had stood her up?

He anxiously waited for a new text from her. This time he would memorize her number. This new way of not memorizing numbers and just using speed dialing was messing with his life.

Back in the days when the phones weren't so convenient, he had memorized all the numbers. Now he was lost. His phone pinged just as he put it down. He grabbed it quickly, but it was a message from Kelsey.

"Do you still do house calls? My niece has a high fever." And with it, she had sent directions to her house.

"Kelsey, Kelsey, Kelsey." Deuce drummed his fingers on the steering wheel.

He didn't want to be seeing Kelsey so often. These days it seemed as if she was everywhere, but he couldn't ignore this text.

Kelsey's sister, Kelly, had two adorable baby girls. The oldest girl, Kira, looked uncannily like Kelsey. Kelly used to joke that he and Kelsey's daughter would look just like her. He had always liked Kelly and her little family. He would do the house call; this was not about Kelsey after all.

He drove up to the apartment building. It was a two-minute walk from Sunrise Medical as Kelsey had said; she was in Town House Four. He took his medical bag with him. Kelsey opened the door before he could use the buzzer.

"Morning Deuce," she said brightly, too brightly for someone who was supposedly the aunt of a sick child. "Kira's temperature is way too high."

"You're babysitting?" Deuce asked.

"Yes," Kelsey said. "I have Kira and Kitana for the weekend. Kelly and Ben went to an all-inclusive hotel. The patient is this way." Kelsey led him through the hallway and into a room.

"Uncle DJ," Kira said brightly when she saw him. She didn't look sick one bit. Deuce looked at Kelsey accusingly. She was using the child to get him to come over to her townhouse, he was sure.

He did the checks though. Kira's temperature was slightly above normal, but it wasn't anything to be alarmed about, he said as much. Kelsey, who had graduated third in their med school batch, put her hand over her heart like a clueless layperson and battered her eyelashes.

"I'm so relieved."

"Do you want some breakfast, Deuce?"

Deuce smiled at Kira, who was quite complicit in this scheme and then glared at Kelsey.

"It was quite shameful of you to use your niece like this," he said, "and no. I do not want any breakfast, but I could do with a cup of peppermint tea."

"Sure," Kelsey said. "This way, do you like the townhouse? It belongs to Ben's sister. She's selling if I want to buy."

"It's nice." Deuce looked around. There was a black and white theme going on and a giant portrait of a lady with juicy red lips to brighten up the space.

"I have a small backyard here and that the kids can play in when they come over?" Kelsey said. Deuce sat at the island and watched as she got the fixings for the tea.

He must be feeling out of sorts because this morning, he was not particularly resentful of Kelsey. She had gotten him to come to her townhouse by using her niece. That was a straight-up Kelsey move, and yet he wasn't angry about it.

"So, do you think I should get it," Kelsey asked. "It's in a nice neighborhood, it's close to Sunrise Medical, it's big enough for our kids or when Kira and Kitty come over.

Deuce shook his head. "Say that again."

"Children." Kelsey crossed her arms, deliberately pushing up her breasts to spill over her tube top. "I want one or two."

"Shouldn't you be telling this to someone you're in a relationship with?" Deuce asked.

"I've always imagined having children with you?" Kelsey said. She placed the peppermint tea in front of him and brushed him with her breast. "Remember how it was between us, Deuce?" Kelsey leaned closer to him. "you and me against the world."

He could smell her perfume. It was light and subtle, and very much like Kelsey. He looked at her lips and remembered how soft they felt against his. He was falling under her spell again. Just then, his phone rang like a slap across his face. What was he doing? He grabbed it so fast he stubbed his finger.

"Hi, DJ. Elsa here," Elsa said cheerfully. "I Whatsapped you an invitation to my house party. You have not replied."

"Er, Elsa," Deuce said. "I didn't have my phone, I lost it and just got back my number this morning."

"Oh, Elsa," said. "Well, in that case, I'll WhatsApp it to you again. Check it. I need to know my final headcount."

"Okay," DJ said. "As soon as I get it, I'll reply." He jumped up from the stool as soon as Elsa hung up, and he backed away from Kelsey. "I am leaving now," he said.

Kelsey, give him a half-smile. "Are you sure you want to leave?"

"Very sure," DJ said.

"Maybe you can come over tonight..." Kelsey suggested. "Oh no, not tonight." She shook her head before he could say no. "I'll have to do three hours up at Golden Acres." She made a face. "I hear my former mother-in-law is living up there now. I hope she's not a patient. That woman hates my guts. Well then, raincheck, tomorrow?"

"What?" Deuce narrowed his eyes at her. "Listen, Kelsey."

"Don't say it," Kelsey said. "It's only a matter of time before we pick up where we left off, and then you and I will be an item again."

Deuce exited the house. He didn't even bother contradicting her. If Elsa hadn't called, he would have succumbed. He was a wuss, and he liked to be tortured, obviously.

"Dani, where are you, text me," he murmured. She was the only one who could set him right.

Chapter Eleven

"We're getting two new staff members today," Stella said tiredly when she joined Danica for lunch in the staff cafeteria, "and we're losing one."

"Who are we losing?" Danica asked tiredly. She wasn't in the best of spirits today. She was feeling down-right unhappy. It was like reading a book that had its last few pages torn out. It was anti-climactic. She felt like a black cloud was hanging over her head. She feared this would be her state for the rest of the week. She was genuinely feeling lost.

"Your girl, Opal." Stella snorted. "She was rude to the wrong person."

"She was?" Danica asked, "but everybody loves her! who was she rude to?"

"Your grand aunt, Florence Jackson." Stella shook her head. "That girl is crazy. How could she not know that Florence Jackson is a board member, and one of the owners of this place, her husband was the original owner."

"I tell you; Opal has gone mad. I am short-staffed as it is," Danica said, "We need more people in the department. The more people keep moving up here, the more demand we will have on the recreation department. It's getting tough keeping up," Danica said bitterly.

"Woah there, mate." Stella looked at her puzzled. "What happened to sunny Danica?"

"I met DJ, that's what happened," Danica growled, "and to say that the meeting was below expectations would be understating it. It was as if he wasn't the one that I was texting. He didn't know key details about me. I tested him by saying that my mother was bedridden and all of that, and he lapped it up. It's just strange and weird."

Stella sighed. "You know, that's one of the things I don't like about online dating or not knowing somebody personally—people lie. They make up stuff to look better. I'm sorry you had a bad experience with this one."

"It's because I've had bad experiences," Danica said, "that is why I chose this method of dating, it doesn't matter if you think you know someone face to face for years. At least with this method of meeting someone, you have to be verified, single, and referred by someone like a clergy before you can sign up with their reference number. This thing is really vetted. There are so many people who have had success with it. Why is it that the lone bad experience would be mine?"

"Nobody tells you about their bad experiences," Stella said. "Usually, people only share the positives. I met this guy over social media. His pictures looked good, there was no photoshopping going on, and I thought that, he was quite to my taste. I met him in person, and he was just as charming as he was when we were texting. We went out on a couple dates, and I was so in love." Stella rolled her eyes. "And then one day we had fish at a restaurant by the beach in Port

Royal, and a lady drove up, headed for our table, pulled a chair, sat at the table and said, 'So why didn't anybody invite me to this date with my husband?'"

Danica gasped.

"That's not all," Stella snorted. "The lady took a gun out of her purse..."

Danica widened her eyes. "You're making this up."

"Oh girl, I wish I was." Stella shook her head. "When the wife started waving the gun around, I saw my life flash before my eyes because that lady looked like she was going to pull the trigger, I tell you."

"And what did you do?" Danica asked.

"My senses kicked in, and I ran, like everybody else, having the presence of mind to grab my purse. Luckily the woman didn't care about me. My date, her husband, was the target. People were yelling, 'call the police!' My date was begging for his life, like a wimp."

"So, what happened next?" Danica asked.

"He was using his children's school money to wine and dine me," Stella said. "and apparently she was the police. She worked at one of the toughest police stations in Kingston, which means she knew what to do with that gun.

"I told you this story to let you know that not all the experiences that we think are tragic really are. It could be worse."

"I believe you," Danica chuckled.

"See, I made you laugh." Stella grimaced. "But enough about me," Stella said. "What really happened with this DJ guy?"

"I didn't like him. I didn't feel it. It's not that he wasn't good looking, it's just that... I don't know. Maybe I'm too shallow."

"You followed your instincts," Stella said. "Do you know

how many mishaps I have escaped because I follow my instincts."

"My mom says it's God's guidance and not my instincts I should follow. She said I should stop moping about it."

Stella shrugged. "Well then, listen to your mom."

"I usually do, especially on these matters," Danica sighed. "She has a story about not following her natural instincts; it's pretty compelling."

"Tell me," Stella leaned forward. "I am all ears."

"My mom moved to the United States, and she found a church in Fort Lauderdale... Church and church life is very important to my mom, and she takes it seriously. She was adopted, you know, by a pastor and his wife. She's a pastor's kid."

"I didn't know that," Stella said. "So, your grandfather is a pastor?"

"Was a pastor," Danica said. "He's retired now. My mother always knew she was adopted. She just never knew who her biological parents were or where to look for them. So four years ago, when I found Giselle, it was mind-blowing."

"I can imagine," Stella said.

"Yes, it was," Danica said. "What was I talking about again?"

"How your mother met your father."

"Yes, my mom said that my dad used to play the piano at church, he had liked her, but she wasn't into him. She was into a tall, dark, and handsome man named Silas, and they dated for a while. In her eyes, Silas was perfect. He was from Jamaica, just like her. My mom is mixed race, black and Indian, and so was Silas. They had similar tastes, etcetera. He was perfect, or so she thought, but the Holy Spirit kept telling her, 'No, Silas is not the one for you.'

"Like the Holy Spirit literally spoke to her?" Stella looked skeptical.

"He did in her case, and my mom said it was like a voice said— Silas is not the one for you, it was very clear and very insistent.

"My mom said she got more of a nudge toward my father, and she couldn't understand why. That wasn't the match she had in her head."

"Anyway, she listened to the voice, broke it off with Silas, and finally gave my father a chance. A year later, they were married, and Silas married someone else a few years later."

"When I was ten, I remember my mother watching the news." Danica shook her head. "Thinking about it now gives me goosebumps."

"Go on," Stella leaned forward eagerly.

"There was this guy on it. He had killed his wife and children and was on the run. Everybody found it shocking, because they seemed to be a happy, normal, loving Christian family."

"Silas?" Stella raised her eyebrows. "It was him, wasn't it?"

"One and the same." Danica sighed. "My mother started crying. I remember it vividly because I couldn't remember seeing her that emotional.

"She kept saying, that could have been me, that could have been me, and then she got down on her knees and started praying, saying, 'Thank you, Lord Jesus. Thank you for saving me.'"

"Did they catch him?" Stella asked.

"Yes, they did," Danica sighed. "He was trying to commit suicide, but it didn't happen. So they caught him before he could make a second attempt and charged him with murder. He killed his family because he was living a double life. He had a boyfriend, and the wife was threatening to expose him."

"My goodness," Stella muttered. "This is a crazy world."

"That is why you have to commit your life to God every single day, and he will direct your paths," Danica said, "And that is the crazy thing. I thought he was directing me to DJ. I felt it, it felt right. I'm not saying you should go off feelings, but it was just perfect. We started talking the minute that we signed up.

"It was as if we signed up at the right time, and we saw each other almost at the same time online. He was reeling from a breakup from someone he called K, and I had once again gone out on a completely disappointing date. I had made up my mind, no marriage, no children. The single life would be for me."

"So cynical at twenty-six." Stella shook her head. "At twenty-six, I was so hopeful." Stella's phone beeped. "That's Pat. I didn't finish preparing the documents for the two new staff members, and I'll have to make space over at the medical center."

"Who are the new staff members?" Danica asked.

"We're getting an ophthalmologist on Tuesdays and Thursdays. A doctor Ryan Greer. He's a widow forty-seven, no kids."

Danica chuckled. "Okay."

"And a rheumatologist, Mondays, and Wednesday. A Dr. Kelsey Channing. She is thirty-four and divorced, no kids, and I don't care whether she is single or not cause she's a girl. I am interested in Ryan Greer. He is finger-licking good looking."

"I thought you described Lee Wiley that way," Danica grinned. "I guess Dr. Ryan Greer has competition in your fantasies?"

"Girl, it's getting crowded up in here. I have to go. I'll

have to show Dr. Kelsey her office. The residents heard she'll be here today, and everyone wants to see her. I think she's booked out until the end of the year. It seems as if everybody has a touch of arthritis or bursitis or osteoporosis. She is the perfect match for the older set, obviously."

"Okay, have fun," Danica said, looking down at her plate. Despite what she had told Stella about listening to her instincts, she was still feeling down. The feeling wasn't quite gone, and she still felt the loss.

****

Kelsey was having a good experience at Golden Acres. They had a small health center that was fairly equipped. They had a full-time nurse on staff and a roster of doctors for various needs. She ran into Ace Jackson when she just arrived, and it hit her afresh, how much Ace and Deuce resembled each other, how handsome they both were, and how stupid she was for letting Deuce go.

She had always been into self-sabotage. She had left Deuce time and time again, but now she realized her mistake. This time was different, she could feel it, and he was weakening. She could feel that too.

She was sure they would be together again, and this time she'd have the family she'd always wanted with him. This time, she was more mature. She had been playing the song this time by John Legend. The line, *'I realize I made a mistake. I thought that I needed some space, but I just let love go to waste. This time I want it all'* kept playing over and over in her head. Those were her sentiments.

She wanted it all, and she wanted it with Deuce.

"I heard you were back," Ace said when he met her at the reception desk.

"I am back and determined to make up for past mistakes," Kelsey said. "Can you put in a word or two for me with Deuce? I know he listens to you."

"Ah, Kelsey," Ace shook his head. "I have learned a long time ago to stay out of you and Deuce's relationship dance."

Kelsey made a face. "You helped me out the first time we broke up."

"That's because Deuce was moping around the place, and it seemed as if it was the end of the world for him, and I hated seeing him in that state," Ace said, "but I have since learned my lesson. You're on your own, Kelsey." He smiled and winked at her.

"Thanks a lot, Ace Jackson."

Ace laughed.

It hadn't been a bad start to the day at all, until now. Kelsey checked the patient file of our next appointment and almost balked at who it was, Leona Julius. There was no love lost between them.

She had spent her first six months in Canada, the length of her marriage to Dale, at Leona's house. It had been six months of pure hell.

Leona had been welcoming at first, but when Kelsey pointed out that Dale was not treating her right, the woman had gone into delusional denial mode.

Leona couldn't stop her— Dale is perfect chorus— long enough to see that her son wasn't acting right.

Maybe she and Dale would have lasted more than the six months if it hadn't been for Leona. She endorsed everything that Dale did. It was as if he had something over his mother. She was an otherwise reasonable woman who lost it when it came to her son.

Leona came into the office and sat before her, giving her a stony glare. "I had to come and see if it was true. That it was really you."

"It is me," Kelsey said.

"I hope you're not up here to try to get back Dale." Leona leaned forward. "He's seeing someone else."

"Is that so?" Kelsey was disinterested. She didn't care who Dale was seeing, or maybe she should care and spare a thought for the unfortunate woman.

"A gorgeous girl who loves him to bits," Leona said.

"Well, I'm happy for him," Kelsey said. "I'm seeing someone else too, someone I shouldn't have stopped seeing in the first place."

"Oh, so you're back with the ex," Leona snarled. "That man is going to need some extra intercessory prayer."

"And so is whoever Dale is with," Kelsey said. "Now that girl is going to need intercessory prayers, psychologists, and a whip to keep him in line. She doesn't realize what a screwed-up man you have grown, Leona."

Leona flinched.

"Oh, that's right. You weren't there for his developing years." Kelsey looked at her balefully. "You left him to be grown by abusive people who messed with his mind. He needs psychological help, Leona, not mommy's constant enabling."

"I never liked you, Kelsey."

"The feeling is mutual," Kelsey smiled. "Was there anything else?"

"No," Leona snarled, "as if I would want you to touch me."

She walked away with her head held high.

Chapter Twelve

The flowers started coming on Tuesday. By Thursday evening, the reception area was inundated with flowers and Danica had taken to carrying them to the residents.

"Dale Julius is wasting his money and time," Danica fumed. He started out with white roses and then started sending red ones.

Her only consolation was that Dale was putting money in Guy Wiley's pocket because the flowers came from his farm store. Guy was her cousin; she didn't want to take away business from him, but the floral gifts were becoming unbearable.

She called Kia after a delivery on Thursday. Dale must have bought all the stock.

"Kiya, is it possible to halt your deliveries?"

Kiya chuckled. "No, it's not possible to halt the deliveries. The customer already paid for the flowers, so I have to send them. I'm sending the latest batch to you this evening,"

"Send them to Ace on your behalf," Danica groaned. "What color flowers are they?"

"Red for love," Kiya chuckled, "thanks for the offer, but today is Thursday, Ace plays tennis with his brother, Deuce every Thursday."

Danica sighed.

"Can you play?" Kiya asked.

"Yes," Danica snorted, "it's my favorite sport. I sometimes pretend that I am Serena Williams when I am hitting the ball all over the court."

Kiya laughed. "We should join them on Thursdays. You and Deuce against me and Ace. It should be fun. I am just learning the game, though, but Ace said I'm a fast learner."

"That should be fun," Danica said. "I keep hearing about Deuce Jackson, maybe I should meet him. Is he single now?"

"The last time I heard." Kiya murmured. "But don't you have a romance going on? Dale Julius seems keen on you. He sent twelve notes with the flowers, he texts us with the lines, and we add them."

"I haven't read them," Danica huffed. "I don't want to read them."

"The guy is pouring his heart out using Brian McKnight songs." Kiya chuckled. "The latest note I am dutifully attaching to this bouquet says— *one, you're like a dream come true, two, just want to be with you, three Danica it's plain to see that you're the only one for me...*"

"I can't believe this," Danica felt herself getting worked up. "He is wasting his money and time. I don't find flowers and chocolates and those kinds of things romantic. Gifts are not my love language. We discussed each other's love language some time ago. We even did the quiz together. Mine was words of affirmation, his was quality time."

"I can't stand him, it's as if he doesn't know me!" Danica

shouted in frustration. "I wasted a year with this idiot. Online dating sucks. It's all a fraud, even Christian Singles. Maybe that one is the biggest fraud of all."

Kiya cleared her throat. "Maybe it's not the site that is the fraud. Maybe it's just him. He texts pieces of the Brian McKnight songs to us and claims it is a poem that he personally wrote. We usually laugh when he sends us another line, but thinking about it now, why lie about such a simple thing?"

"I don't know," Danica said. "He's creepy, and I want nothing to do with him again."

"Well, if you feel uncomfortable," Kiya said, "I'll tell him that we can't fulfill any more of his orders if they are going to you. If you feel that this is stalking, you probably should tell the police."

"No, I don't," Danica said. "It's just that I thought we had something going. I never met him before, but when I did, I felt as if something wasn't right. I confided quite a bit of stuff to him before I met him, but now, I really don't like him. I don't feel it. So now, I feel kind of guilty like, you know, I'm the one who lost the plot."

"You should be able to change your mind if you want to," Kiya said, "and don't feel guilty about it."

"Thanks, Kiya," Danica said. "My mom said the same thing this week."

"I'll ask Ace about this tennis match," Kiya said before she hung up. "Maybe meeting other people will take your mind off this."

Danica hung up, she doubted that. Her mind would never be at peace again. She hadn't realized how invested she had been in the online relationship until now.

She knew what the root cause of all of this was, she had told DJ too many things about herself. She might not have gone into some personal details, like where she lived and that kind of thing, but she had really laid it all out to him.

That was the crux of her discomfort. She had thought that he had laid it all out to her too, but that was obviously a lie.

She needed to spend a weekend away from Golden Acres, especially this weekend. She didn't want to run into Dale Julius and his mother.

She walked toward the staff housing. It was less glamorous than where the residents lived, but it was still lovely. The rooms reminded her of her college dorm room. She hardly stayed there, and she was considering giving it up and move to stay with her aunt, Florence, full time.

Aunt Florence only asked her to stay every day.

Danica chuckled to herself. She had gone from being the only child of only children to having a large and interesting family.

At Elsa and Mason's wedding, she had seen just how large her family was but from a distance. She had spent most of her time hiding out in the car because she had broken out into hives. She had inadvertently eaten something with milk from the night before. She had not been a pretty sight the day after, and she was not in any of Elsa's pictures.

Her face had been swollen, welt filled, and blotchy, and she couldn't have hidden it with makeup.

She was digging for her key to open the apartment door when she heard a distinct clearing of the throat behind her.

She spun around. It was Leona Julius.

"How are you, Danica?" Leona smiled at her, but it didn't reach her eyes.

"I am good," Danica nodded. What she really wanted to ask Leona was, what are you doing here?

She refrained from doing so though.

"Is there something I can help you with, Mrs. Julius?"

Leona narrowed her eyes at the formality, the last time they spoke, she had been Leona.

"My son tells me that you are ignoring him. Is there something wrong?"

"Yes," Danica nodded. "I am not interested in him after meeting him."

"That's fair enough. It is a free country and a person is entitled to change her mind." Leona nodded. "But why? I don't understand it. Dale is hurting at this rejection, and it hasn't escaped me that you are giving his floral gifts to everybody. That is cold and mean."

Danica sighed. "Sorry, Mrs. Julius, this is between your son and me."

Leona nodded. "I understand that, but at the same time, you should understand that when my child is hurting, I hurt. At least talk to him, he is not a monster."

Danica felt guilty. She missed the memory of the DJ who she texted on the phone.

"Okay," she sighed. "I'll talk to him."

"He is asking you to meet him at the Chocolat at seven." Leona smiled. "I am happy that you reconsidered."

Danica nodded and watched Leona's retreating back as she glided down the steps to toward the recreation center.

Maybe she had been too quick to judge DJ. She let herself into the apartment, changed into her tracksuit, and did what she usually did when her heart felt heavy; she went walking.

It was the best time for her to meditate. She took her usual path. She had to cross the recreational center and the parking lot. That's where the hardest trail was, and she needed a hard trail right now. She wanted her heart rate to be up and pumping.

She wanted to remember all the things that she had told DJ and other things that he told her. She had told him that she was an only child and that she was her parent's miracle baby. Her mother had been pregnant with twins, and one died.

He knew she had self-esteem issues while growing up. She had told him about the attempted rape. She had told him about her first kiss at church camp because of a dare, and how even though everyone said it wouldn't happen it was just a myth, her braces had somehow gotten tangled up with her partners.

It was the most embarrassing moment of her life to date. He had told her that his most embarrassing moment was when he had just learned to swim and was showing off at a pool party and almost drowned.

She had thought that they would click on meeting face to face. Basically, she had told him everything, and now she was a fool.

Everybody had warned her about this. You never know who you are talking to online.

Now here she was full of regrets and being inundated with flowers and motherly intervention. Leona Julius had just guilted her into seeing DJ and now thinking about it she was recoiling.

What kind of a man sent his mother to intercede on his behalf?

She was almost on our way across the parking lot when she saw the new female doctor, Kelsey Channer. She was on the phone and running her slender fingers through her short blond curls.

Danica looked at her enviously. She wished she had the confidence to dye her hair blonde. The one time she had messed with her hair she was fifteen. She had broken out into one of her worst allergic reaction and had to be taken to the emergency room.

So no dyes for her. Ever.

The doctor was obviously talking to a man. There was a certain lilt to her voice, and she was l, even though nightly rubbing her neck and biting her lips even though no one was watching.

Danica was close enough to hear her say, "I know Thursdays are your tennis time with Ace, but I have a lot of food, DJ, trust me. I have no one else to share it with. I could come over when you guys are finished."

Danica stopped.

This was Deuce Jackson's girlfriend? He must have answered favorably because she looked up with a beatific smile on her face.

She got into her car eagerly, not even realizing that Danica was standing there. A shaft of pain hit Danica out of nowhere. It was as if her heart did an anxious squeeze.

Maybe it was the name DJ, it triggered something in her. She was actually jealous!

"Why am I feeling like this, Lord?" She whispered. She didn't get a response, but the feeling lingered.

Chapter Thirteen

"**S**o, Kelsey is working hard to be in your good graces again." Ace laughed at his brother. They were walking down the stairwell as their usual warm-up exercise. "And you're playing hard to get."

Deuce grimaced. "I am not playing, Ace. This is not like the other times. I had a rough week, and I'm feeling out of sorts."

"You still haven't heard from that text pal of yours?" Ace asked.

"Not a word." Deuce sighed. "She abandoned me. Every day for eighteen months we said something to each other and then I lost my phone. I got back my number but nothing, not a peep from her. It's strange."

"Maybe her phone was lost too," Ace said. "I can't believe you still feel this way about her. I must admit that I never thought you were so serious about this whole online thing."

"It wasn't a conventional relationship, but it was

something," Deuce sighed, "and now it's gone. I've been feeling bereft all week."

"Even with Kelsey on your case?" Ace asked.

"Especially with Kelsey on my case."

They played, but Deuce's heart wasn't in it. Usually, Ace wouldn't win so easily. After another dismal set from him, Ace sat at courtside.

"Listen, DJ. I know I'm not the best person to be giving you advice about relationships and such, but I have to say, if God wants you to be with someone, he'll make it happen at the right time and with the right person. Don't force it, whether it's with Kelsey, or your text pal or whomever. I learned this when I was hung up on Lucia, but now that I've met Kiya, I'm like Lucia who."

"You two do seem to suit each other," Deuce said, "And thanks for the advice, bro. I'm not forcing anything. Just feeling a little messed up from being ghosted. As for Kelsey, I am treading cautiously where she is concerned. I would rather she not be in this discussion at all."

****

Kelsey had been to his apartment before. He had bought the place a week before they broke up the last time.

"Maybe I should get an apartment here," Kelsey said when he answered the door. "It's nicer than I remembered."

"The last time you were here, you said it was too big and that I was only getting it to force you to have a baby."

"I was paranoid, and I'm sorry." Kelsey smiled. "You have to admit, that was all you spoke about at one time, marriage and babies. It was frightening."

"But I'm not talking about it now," Deuce said, "so there no need to be frightened. Come on in."

He closed the door behind her, and Kelsey laid out the food on the kitchen counter.

"I have chicken fish, beef, you name it. My mother catered for a large party, and she dumped all of the excess on me."

"How is your mom?" Deuce asked.

"She still thinks I'm crazy for breaking up with you." Kelsey smiled at him wryly. "You know she was your number one fan."

"I take it she didn't warm up to Dale."

"Nope," Kelsey said. "She hated him, begged me not to marry him, which sort of made him more attractive to me. I think that is why I said yes to his proposal."

"Ah," Deuce smirked. "I thought your mother had mastered reverse psychology with you by now. You always did the opposite of what she asks."

"I wonder why that is," Kelsey scrunched up her face and tapped her chin.

"You were a rebellious, obstinate child, and you grew up to be a rebellious, obstinate adult." Deuce raised a brow. "How is Michael, your long-suffering stepfather?"

"Good. Kelsey grinned. "I recently apologized to him for being a terror when I was younger. He said he was hoping that I would marry a man who had children and become a stepmother and that one of the children would be a Kelsey."

"You would know what it feels like." Deuce laughed. "Maybe he will still get his wish."

"No," Kelsey looked at him as if he were insane. "You don't have any children, ergo I cannot be a stepmother."

"But, you and I are not getting married," Deuce said good-naturedly. "We did that dance already, where I asked, and you turned me down."

Deuce realized he was hungry. He piled his plate high and sat at the dining room table. He opened the patio doors so they could have a view of the sea.

"That was the old Kelsey, new Kelsey would give anything to hear you ask her again." Kelsey filled her plate with food. "New Kelsey is not afraid to beg and grovel and ask for forgiveness."

Deuce didn't respond. He didn't feel like arguing. He didn't feel much of anything, he realized suddenly. The thought of Kelsey groveling and begging filled him with indifference. He didn't care anymore.

Kelsey sat across from him, and he looked on her pretty face, that face that had caused him a world of pain.

She stared back at him and then began to smile. "What is it?"

"Nothing," Deuce said faintly, nothing was the right response, he was feeling nothing.

"This is just like old times," Kelsey said happily. "You and I having a meal after a day of work or study. Then after this… "

"No, it's not like old times." Deuce interrupted her. "Everything is different."

"We'll see about that." Kelsey smiled at him slyly.

Chapter Fourteen

Danica was sweating profusely even though the evening was chilly. She had walked so fast up the hiking trail that the cold mountain air had no effect on her. She was dreaming of a cold shower, as cold as she could stand it. She had walked for clarity, but she was more confused than ever.

She couldn't remember ever feeling jealous of anyone, and she had been jealous of Kelsey Channer. A woman she had only met in passing and all because she had a boyfriend named DJ.

She felt gross inside. She was never one to covet anyone, but here she was practically green with it.

She quickly let herself inside her apartment and had a cold shower. She was in the mood to just stay in and stew over her lot in life, but she had promised to meet Dale at the Chocolat. It was the fanciest restaurant at Golden Acres and required fancy dress. She had eaten there once with her grandmother and grand aunt.

Her grandmother, Heather Greyson, was married to possibly the richest man in Jamaica, Edmond Midas Greyson, and she was doing the rounds renewing contacts with the family and trying to get to know them all.

Danica headed to the tiny closet and pulled out the dress that she had worn the last time. It was a royal blue dress that fitted her hourglass figure snuggly, but it wasn't too tight.

She left her hair out; it was a mixture of curls and waves which hit her at her waist. She rarely let her hair down these days, but as a teenager, she had used it as camouflage, trying to hide her face, hoping that people would stare at her hair and not at her unfortunate, mottled face.

She was a confident woman now with not a spot in sight, except for that mole under her chin.

She did a spin in the floor-length mirror, grinning like a Cheshire cat, and then she remembered that she was going on a dinner date with DJ, and her grin disappeared.

Her phone pinged at the same time that she picked up her purse, and she checked her message.

It was from Elsa. *Don't forget the party this Sunday.*

Danica texted back, *I won't.* She added a smiley face, and then she checked her affirmation of the day from Miranda. She had barely glanced at it this morning.

Since she had stopped sending them to DJ, she didn't read them with the same kind of eagerness that she had in the past.

It read: *Sometimes life gives you a second chance because you weren't ready the first time.*

Okay, this was her second chance with DJ; she was going to swallow whatever misgivings she had and go with the flow.

****

It wasn't working out. He was charming and affable. He

smelled good, and he looked handsome in his suit, the waitress was flirting with him big time but that gag reflex that she had felt the first time she met him was still there.

It was a no.

"God gave people the gag reflex for a reason." Danica heard her mother's voice in her head. "Ignore it at your peril."

He ordered cheesecake for dessert, and then she knew it was over. He should know about her dairy allergies. She couldn't have cheesecake. She allowed the waitress to bring it and then she watched him eat his. She had to admit it looked divine, and he was certainly enjoying his.

"Why aren't you eating?" He asked innocently.

"Because I have a dairy allergy." Danica narrowed her eyes at him. "Did you ever read any of my texts?"

"Oh," he guiltily cleared his throat. "I may have forgotten a thing or two. I have a memory issue."

"A memory issue?" Danica raised her eyebrow.

"Yes," Dale nodded, "brought on by emotional problems relating to my ex-wife."

"You were married?" Danica widened her eyes. "You never said you were married."

"She is in the past." He said flippantly.

"But…" Danica narrowed her eyes and looked at him. "You said you have never tied the knot. Ever. You are a liar."

"I am?" Dale shook his head, "no, I am not. I just don't remember things. Well, if I said that I must have…"

Danica glared at him. "I don't see any use in us continuing this charade, DJ."

Dale grimaced. "I would much prefer it if you called me Dale."

"Well, Dale," Danica said, a finality to her tones that made him still and tense up as if he were anticipating a blow. "I don't want to do dinners again or write to you again. I feel hoodwinked, deceived."

"I understand." Dale reached across the table and held her hand. "What if I told you I was different when I wrote those things. I am a completely different person now."

"I would say," Danica pulled her hand from his. "Then I am sorry about that. I quite liked the DJ who wrote to me."

She got up. "I have to go."

"Wait!" Dale said, "your cheesecake!"

"Have it." Danica turned around and glared at him. "And after this, leave me alone. Stop sending me flowers and the words to Brian McKnight's songs. I don't like you!"

The whole restaurant heard, and there were quite a few patrons there. Dale shrank in his chair.

Chapter Fifteen

Elsa and Mason knew how to throw a party. It seemed as if they had invited most persons from each side of their families. Well, most of those who were living in Kingston. When Elsa had said it was going to be an intimate party of close family and friends, she had assumed that maybe twenty persons would be there, but this intimate party had nearly a hundred persons.

It was under a tent on the lawn below Mason's house. It had the same view as Golden Acres'. The weather was perfect for the party, she remarked as much to Kiya, and the flowers were lovely.

"I had nothing to do with the flowers," Kiya grinned. "This was all Celia Jackson and her Garden Club."

"You're getting on with her yet?" Danica asked.

"Surprisingly, yes," Kiya said. "We speak the universal language of plants. She has even taken to dropping by the farm store to chat ever so often."

"Great," Danica said. "It's always good to get on with the mother-in-law."

"She's not the mother-in-law yet, but the possibility is creeping closer and closer, whenever Ace and I hang out it is getting harder and harder to say goodbye." Kiya chuckled. "How are you doing? How is that guy? The one that you met, the one that was sending you flowers."

Danica made a face. "I spoke to him. We hung out one evening and I asked him to stop sending me flowers, so he stopped.

"He calls me and then hangs up, but I know it's him. He's using a different number, but I can hear him breathing in the phone."

"He's weird," Kiya said. "That just goes to show that no matter the profession, a person can act the fool."

"True," Danica grimaced.

Elsa came over to them and hugged her. "Cousin! I know I've been scarce."

"I understand," Danica hugged her back. "You're in honeymoon bliss with your love."

Elsa looked over at Mason and blushed. He was in deep conversation with one of his family members. He looked over at her at the same time and then winked.

Elsa blew a kiss after him.

"Oh, to be in love," Kiya grinned.

Ace waved her over to where he was, and she excused herself. "Speak to you later, Danica."

"You and Kiya make me sick," Danica said mournfully. "The two of you are living a romance novel. I am living in a horror movie."

"You have got to update me on what is going on," Elsa said. "I have not heard from you since you met DJ. Was he all that you expected him to be?

" No, he wasn't," Danica frowned. "But I don't want to burden you with my troubles and hog all your attention away from your guests."

"It's a family party," Elsa snorted, "everybody knows everybody else. Let's go to the living room. It's quiet in there."

Elsa pulled her across the lawn and into her spacious home and garden kitchen before she could protest. It was bustling with the caterer and her staff who were still arranging things to bring out to the food tent.

"So," Elsa said, sitting in one of the comfortable overstuffed settees. "Talk to me."

Danica looked around. "I like the decor in here."

Elsa giggled. "I had bookmarked this decor in a magazine, and Mason found it and used it."

"You guys have such a lovely story," Danica said.

"You will have your own story one day," Elsa said. "To tell you the truth, I wasn't holding out hope that this text-pal-business would have worked. How many people do you know that this sort of thing works for? It's hard enough having a relationship with people that you know and see all the time, much less a faceless stranger who will give you a convenient account of himself." Elsa shook her head. "The world is crazy."

"I genuinely thought it would have worked," Danica said. "I mistakenly thought that I could feel the chemistry even though we hadn't seen each other face to face."

"You'll meet someone, someday," Elsa said gently, "and this whole episode will be a footnote in your life.

****

Deuce was on his way to Elsa and Mason's party. If he hadn't promised to go, he wouldn't have. He felt a little down and despondent. The last thing he wanted to do right now was go to a party. It was a testament to his state of mind that when his phone rang, he didn't even look to see who the caller was.

He was sorry he answered when Kelsey said chirpily in his ear. "Hey, Deuce."

"Kelsey," he said without much emotion in his voice.

"I am in a pickle," Kelsey said, sounding like someone who wasn't in a pickle at all. He didn't want to ask how he could help her out, so he just let her speak.

"I came to Benji's by the Sea to drop off a cake for my mother. Someone is having a birthday party down here, and when I went back to my car, it wouldn't start."

"Call a wrecker," Deuce said sullenly.

"I called my mechanic," Kelsey said, her voice exasperated. "He said he would reach here in three hours. He is doing some other job. You live close by, so I called you. I can't be standing out here alone when my dear friend lives so close. I was wondering if I could come and chill out with you for a couple hours until he gets here."

"No can do," DJ said, "I have a party."

"Come on, DJ. Help me out," Kelsey said. "I'm not a monster, you know. I thought we were making progress, weren't we? Where is your party?"

"At Mason's place in the hills, near Golden Acres,"

"Ah," Kelsey said. "Can I come? I'll just sit in the car and wait. Anything is better than just standing around out here."

Deuce sighed. He knew a bid for attention when he heard it. He just didn't have the energy to fight Kelsey today. "Well, I guess you can come," Deuce said.

"Yay, thank you so much, Deuce."

Deuce drove towards Benji's by the Sea. At this time on a

Sunday, with a lovely afternoon like this, the place was jam-packed with cars. Kelsey was waiting for him at the front of the restaurant in a blue and white sundress and matching sandals. She looked as if she was dressed for the party.

She looked fresh and pretty, he grudgingly admitted. He stopped, and she came into the car, smiling.

"Thanks a bunch, DJ. Believe it or not, I did not orchestrate this moment. I actually called a taxi."

"And?" Deuce raised an eyebrow.

"They said they'd send a car in an hour and a half. But when I thought about it, I would have to be down here to let my mechanic into my car."

"What a conundrum," Deuce said.

Kelsey ignored his sarcasm.

"And that is why I called you because I knew you lived close by. So whose party are we going to?"

"Elsa and Mason's. Remember my cousin, Mason?"

"Oh, yes." Kelsey nodded. "Your advertising cousin, Mr. Quiet. I've always gotten the feeling that Mason doesn't like me."

"Then this will be awkward," Deuce said, "bringing you to his party."

He turned on the radio to discourage further conversation.

Kelsey looked at him and grinned, "I can take a hint."

"What did you say?" Deuce asked, turning up the volume on the music that was playing.

"I said," Kelsey shouted, "I can take a hint. I promise not to bore you with conversation if you turn down the volume!"

Deuce turned the volume at a reasonable level and glanced at Kelsey, "thank you for not being obtuse."

They traveled in relative silence until Luther Vandross' I'd Rather came on.

Kelsey turned to him, her eyes alight with unspoken

emotions. "This is our song, DJ. I can't tell you how many times in the past year I've sang this, thinking it was my sentiment to you."

Deuce glanced at her and then shook his head. "It is the opposite of what you used to do."

She turned up the volume and started singing.

I can't blame you if you turn away from me, like I've done you, I can only prove the things I say with time, Please be mine...

Deuce winced; Kelsey did not have the best singing voice, but she didn't care.

She looked at him when it was over. "I meant every word, DJ."

"And I am genuinely indifferent," Deuce said flatly.

Kelsey smiled, "I can feel you softening toward me."

"If we got back into a relationship, I would need my head examined." Deuce glanced at her and then back at the road.

"I've done brain surgery before, granted it wasn't on a human being, it was on a pig," Kelsey said, "but I would be extra careful in examining your brain."

Deuce almost cracked a smile. He was softening. He shouldn't be bringing her to Mason's party and laughing at her jokes.

"I will pay you to shut up." He finally grumbled.

They arrived at the party, and it seemed as if Deuce was the last one to get there.

"I'll just stay the right here," Kelsey said. She sounded forlorn like she wanted him to invite her inside.

He didn't want to invite her in. He didn't want his family speculating that they were together again.

"I won't be long," he said. "I never stayed for the reception, you know, I had to go to an emergency. It would look odd for me not to come to this party."

He headed toward the sign that said, 'To the Party'. It had an arrow that was pointing toward the back of the house. He passed his father on the way.

"I am just going to get my camera," Ace senior said, "my old point-and-shoot does a better job than my phone."

Deuce chuckled. His father didn't like modern technology and still had a hard time letting go of his old stuff.

"Do they still have those camera places where you go to get your film developed?" Deuce chuckled. "Is that the type of camera you have, Dad."

"They still have a place like that," Ace Senior muttered, "and I see you laughing, Deuce. Everything comes back in style, mark my words."

Deuce laughed outright. It felt good. His life had been too serious lately.

It was a larger crowd than he had anticipated. And it was all family, it seemed. He recognized nearly all the faces, except for one.

There was a girl walking with Elsa from the direction of the house. Her skin looked luminous in the golden afternoon light.

She was laughing at something that Elsa said, and she seemed so happy that it made him smile. He couldn't remember the last time he smiled, just watching someone smiling. She stopped him in his tracks.

"Your mouth is opened," Ace said, somewhere behind him.

"No, it's not," Deuce protested, but he didn't want to look away from where she was. "Who is she?"

"That's Danica," Ace said, "Our most popular staff member at Golden Acres. She has the personality to match the face."

"Ah," Deuce said incoherently. He was just staring at Danica. She must have felt his stare because she stopped too and stared at him.

"What are you waiting for?" Deuce asked. "When are you going to introduce us?"

"And there I was thinking that you were brokenhearted because you could not get in touch with your text pal." Ace shook his head. "Men are so fickle. Speaking of fickle," Ace whistled, "you brought Kelsey?"

Deuce dragged his eyes from Danica and looked around at his brother. "How do you know that?"

"Because she's over there talking to Dad."

Deuce groaned. "Her car broke down. I picked her up on the way here."

"How convenient," Ace murmured. "Kelsey has always known how to play you."

Deuce grunted. When he swung around to look for Danica, she was no longer where he last saw her. He inexplicably felt bereft.

"Where did she go?" He asked Ace.

"No need to panic, Mr. Loverman." Ace grinned. "She's over there. Come on, let me introduce you two."

Deuce eagerly headed for Danica, but on his way, he was stopped by Kelsey, who wound her hand through his.

"I hope you don't mind, Honey. Your father insisted that I come and join the party. I was sort of hungry, and he said there's much food here. So here I am."

Deuce tried to disentangle himself from Kelsey's clutches, but they were almost where Danica was standing. She was looking at him, drinking him in just as he was doing to her.

"Danica Hunt, this is Deuce Jackson or DJ for short," Ace said.

Deuce's eyes clung to hers. "Nice to meet you, Danica."

"Same here, DJ."

"And I'm Kelsey," Kelsey said, butting into the moment. "Dr. Kelsey Channer."

Danica dragged her eyes from his.

"Er, I have seen you around," she said, "You work at Golden Acres sometimes."

"Yes, I do," Kelsey said brightly. "I haven't had the chance to meet all the staff, yet." She said staff with a little inflection as if she was putting down Danica.

Two thoughts kept ricocheting in Deuce's head while he watched the exchange.

For one, Danica felt familiar. He couldn't quite put his finger on why, and two Kelsey was infuriating him so much that for the first time in years, he felt a genuine revulsion toward her.

He suddenly wished that he didn't know her.

Danica watched the interplay between Deuce and Kelsey with a sick dread. *So this was Kelsey's DJ.*

Deuce forcefully dragged his hands from Kelsey's. He didn't care how it looked. She was trying to make them appear as if they were a couple, and he was having none of that, not when he was feeling this way about Danica Hunt.

When Danica had first seen him, she had gasped, the reaction was so unlike her. She cleared her throat. "Excuse me," she said it as brightly as she could, and then headed back toward the house.

It was just her luck that she had been text pals with the wrong DJ because this one was giving her all the right signals. He was the one that felt right.

Chapter Sixteen

"**I** thought you weren't going to stay at this party for long," Kelsey murmured. She was acting irritable since the moment they left the party, and Deuce had an idea why that was. He had practically ignored her since he met Danica. He had been in deep thought ever since. Danica had taken pains to avoid him during the evening, which in itself was intriguing.

While driving down, it had slowly dawned on him that his text pal's name was Dani, it only needed the CA. Maybe it was wishful thinking because he wanted his text pal to contact him again, and he wanted it to be Danica. He wracked his brain for the many descriptions Dani gave him about herself. She had said she was average looking. Danica wasn't average looking. Dani had mentioned that guys liked her shape. Danica had the kind of shape that gave men whiplash.

"You are not listening to me!" Kelsey intruded on this thought. He glanced at her absentmindedly.

"You know, that's actually true. I wasn't listening. I was thinking about Danica," he said, honestly.

"I knew it," Kelsey whined. "I could see it. You look at her like how you used to look at me."

"That's nonsense," Deuce said, "and none of this is your business."

"Of course, this is my business," Kelsey said. "You are my business. I've loved you since we were very young, and I still love you," Kelsey said, "besides, didn't you have an imaginary friend that was supposed to replace me?"

"My friend is not imaginary," Deuce said ruefully. "You know, I've been thinking about this, and I think we just met her this evening."

Kelsey looked at him as if he were crazy. "Are you taking narcotics?"

"No, but I've been talking to Danica for a year and some months now, and I think I just met her."

"What kind of ridiculous nonsense are you on about?" Kelsey asked.

"You wouldn't understand," Deuce said, "and I'm not about to explain it to you." He slowed down in front of Benji's. "I think this is your stop."

Kelsey snorted.

"Maybe you should call your mechanic," Deuce said. "It has been three hours."

"There was nothing wrong with my car," Kelsey glared at him, "I just wanted to spend some time with you. There is no reason for you to be acting this coldly towards me, Deuce, no reason at all."

"Kelsey," Deuce said, adopting a no-nonsense tone. "I'm going to say this only once. It is over. It is done."

"It is not over or done between us," Kelsey said. "You're still mad at me because I got married to Dale Julius, and that is why you're even inventing a friendship with a girl you just met. You and I will never be done, DJ. Your ego is just hurt, and I'm trying to make it up to you. Remember, when we promised to love each other forever. I want that DJ back. I want you back." Tears gathered in her eyes.

Deuce sighed. "Kelsey, this conversation is three years too late. Please don't call me again."

"Danica will not be the one," Kelsey huffed. "I don't care who she is or where she's from; she is not going to be the one that will be your wife."

She slammed the door and flounced off to the parking lot. Deuce checked his rearview mirror and then drove off.

He was used to little scenes like this from Kelsey, and it was getting old. Frankly, he thought they had gotten past this.

In the past, he would have called her when he got home after realizing how much he couldn't live without her. Today, he was feeling nothing except a deep curiosity.

If Danica is Dani, why had she stopped texting him?

****

Deuce called Ace as soon as he reached home. He hadn't even let himself into his apartment before he was dialing his brother's number.

"Do you have Danica's number?" Deuce asked urgently.

Ace chuckled. "I am driving, and I have you on speakerphone. Kiya can hear you sounding desperate."

"Hey, Kiya," Deuce said.

Kiya giggled. "Hi, DJ."

"I am not desperate," Deuce said, feeling a need to explain himself. "I have a sneaking suspicion that Danica is my text pal."

"No, she is not," Kiya said. "She met her text pal. He has been sending her flowers all week, but Danica doesn't like him.

Deuce felt deflated when he heard that.

"I was so sure," he said, his voice sounded forlorn. "I wanted her number to find out why is it that she stopped texting me?"

"This means a lot to you, doesn't it?" Ace said sympathetically.

"You think?" Deuce said. "I'm left in limbo."

"But you like Danica, anyway, didn't you?" Ace probed.

"It was instant," Deuce said sheepishly. "I guess that's why I wanted her to be my text pal."

"There is no harm in calling her," Ace said. "Wait a sec, let me text you her number. I'll have to stop."

"Good. Thanks, Ace," Deuce said. It was the longest two minutes of his life while he waited for Ace to text him the number. Deuce wasted no time to call it. He called twice, and both times the phone rang without an answer. He got up and paced and then called again.

"Listen to me, Dale Julius," Danica said in his ear. "I'm going to say this once, and you're going to hear me, or else I'm going to call the police."

Deuce widened his eyes. "Stop calling me, stop stalking me, stop sending me flowers, stop putting notes under my aunt's door. Stop it. This is beyond annoying. I met you, and I decided that I don't like you. It's as simple as that. Deal with it!"

Danica hung up before Deuce could say hello.

"Dale Julius!" It didn't take Deuce two minutes to figure out precisely what happened.

Dale had somehow gotten his phone, maybe he had stolen it, and had pretended to be the DJ that Danica was speaking to, and she didn't like him. Deuce started laughing. That is why he had never heard from her again.

He grabbed his car keys. He was going to Golden Acres, calling Danica now would do no good.

****

It took him thirty minutes to get back to Elsa and Mason's place. The party was over, and a cleaning crew was doing the rounds.

"What's up Deuce? Left something?" Elsa asked him when he stepped out of the car.

"Do you know where Danica would be right now?" Deuce asked Elsa. She narrowed her gaze at him.

"Why?"

"It's complicated," Deuce said, "but I think that she is my text pal."

"I knew it," Elsa said excitedly. "I knew it. How did this Dale Julius guy get involved?"

"He stole my phone," Deuce said.

Elsa's grin widened.

"Danica left shortly after you left. She usually spends Sunday nights at Aunt Florence."

Deuce nodded. "Well, okay then." Deuce drove up to Golden Acres. Everything was making sense to him now. He remembered texting Dani, and she had said she was looking for her family, and then she had written to tell him that she had found them.

Why hadn't he linked this with the fact that his Aunt Florence, his uncle's wife, had found her family as well? It was all so plain. And then she said she had worked as a recreation director. And Danica was the head of the entertainment at Golden Acres.

She was in his vicinity all this time. After a week of driving himself crazy because of the lack of communication, he had finally found her. He grinned to himself. Meeting her had been everything he had expected and more.

It was amazing that she was the one that he had been talking to all this time. He drove up to Florence's cottage, and he couldn't wait to get out of the car. There was a light in the living room, but he couldn't see in there clearly. He knocked on the door. He fully expected his aunt to answer, but Danica answered the door instead.

"Deuce," she said huskily. She was still in the same clothes from earlier, her hair looked like she had run her hand through it several times.

Deuce smiled at her. "Is Aunt Florence in?"

"Er. no." Danica was staring at him too. "She left the party with her sister; they are going to some event or the other in Montego Bay tomorrow."

"That's your grandmother, right?" Deuce said.

Danica nodded mutely. Her hand trembled as she pushed a lock of hair behind her ears. *So he had an effect on her.* Deuce gave her a slow, sizzling smile.

She rubbed her neck nervously.

"I, er... do you want to come in?" Danica asked.

Deuce smiled. "Do I make you nervous?"

"No," she laughed nervously.

"I thought you said you were average looking," Deuce murmured, "and that you had bad acne when you were young, and you were bullied in school, and you covered your social awkwardness by being outgoing and out there."

Danica opened her mouth.

"I thought you said after that guy attacked you a couple years ago, that you felt nervous being alone with men."

"I've only told those things to DJ," Danica whispered.

"You love Indian food, long walks in the hills. You come to Jamaica every chance you get because you feel as if you have an affinity with this place.

"Your date to the prom was with a guy from your church. Your parents paid him to take you. Your first kiss was with another little guy who wore braces, and your mouths got tangled together. You meditate every morning when you walk. You send me daily affirmations. I haven't gotten any all week. I miss them."

"How is this possible?" Danica whispered. "How is this... I was sitting on the patio fantasizing about you."

"Me?" Deuce raised an eyebrow. "What about me?"

"I can't tell you," Danica blushed. "I met you earlier, and I was saying, 'Lord, I wish he was the DJ that I was corresponding with.'"

"I am," Deuce said.

"But Dale Julius," Danica shook her head. "I don't understand."

"It seems as if he stole my phone, but I got back my number. And that's when I met you today and decided to call you, but you didn't allow me to get a word in." Deuce grinned. "You need to tell me what Dale Julius has been up to."

"I will, I will," Danica said, "come on in."

"You sure?" Deuce asked.

"I am sure," Danica said happily. "I am not uncomfortable around you. Well, not in a you creep me out kind of way."

Deuce step over the threshold and Danica turned to him and walked right into his arms.

"I'm glad it is you," she whispered.

"Me too." Deuce hugged her closer and inhaled the scent of her hair.

Chapter Seventeen

Deuce was too keyed up to sleep when he left Golden Acres at two in the morning. It was kind of surreal to think that he had finally met Dani, but it almost didn't happen. If circumstances were different, she would have probably met and liked Dale Julius, and he would be out in the cold.

As it was, their long-distance text relationship had proven to be stronger than any of them thought it would be. He liked her, and he wished he didn't have to leave. He felt like a giddy teenager. They had spoken way up into the night.

They stared a lot at each other, so he figured they were both reveling in the fact that they were seeing each other face to face and liked what they saw. He parked his car, got out and almost stopped in his tracks when he saw Dale Julius in the lobby.

"You!" Deuce shouted, "what are you doing here?"

The security at the front desk looked between the two of them. He was on the alert. The truth was Deuce hadn't thought about Dale Julius all evening, but now, he was thinking about him and what he did.

"I live here now!" Dale Julius snorted. "I'm renting a place on the sixth floor."

Deuce looked at him, incredulously, "That is my floor. What are you doing? Stalking me?"

"Don't be ridiculous," Dale said. "Dr. Fenty's wife owns an apartment here, and she knows I was looking for a place to live that is close enough to my mother at Golden Acres and not horrendous long to get to from work. Besides, it's a lovely place by the seaside. Trust me, Deuce, it's quite a coincidence that I'm living here with you."

"Did you steal my phone?" Deuce asked, not mincing words.

"Me, steal!" Dale Julius said incredulously. "Listen. I am an upstanding Christian man, and I belong to a very respectable profession."

Deuce snorted. "Cut the crap! I met Danica today, and I heard you were posing as me."

"She liked you, didn't she?" Dale said, a defeated sound to his voice.

"Oh, yes, she did." Deuce nodded, "and I like her."

"I knew you'd like her," Dale said. "She's pretty and sexy. She is really sexy."

"I liked her before I met her, but of course you will not understand that," Deuce said. "You know, I could have called you many things, but thief was not a name that I would readily assign to you."

"I didn't steal your phone," Dale said. "I was talking to your father, and it fell out of your car when you went to the office to pick up something. I picked it up, told your dad I was good to give it to you, but I was called away. While I was on my way, I saw a text from Dani to you, and it got me thinking. She knew you as DJ. I had the same initials. And so I never bothered to give you back your stupid phone.

"You can have it. It's upstairs. I don't want it for anything else. I thought you would've sorted out the lost phone thing sooner than you did."

Deuce looked at him in horror. "And that's your excuse. You found my phone and then decided to throw in some deception. You could have cost me a relationship with somebody I like."

"You always win," Dale snorted. He jabbed the elevator button. "But I think I'm softening up Danica. After all, she met me first."

"She doesn't like you," Deuce said. "Stay away from her."

Dale stepped into the elevator and gave him a baleful look. "We'll see about that. We'll see which DJ she ends up choosing."

Deuce sighed. He went to another elevator and pushed the button. He was living in the same building as the monster. Was any of this even a coincidence. Dale Julius seemed to pick up where he left off. The envy in the man was real, and Deuce had no idea if he should be concerned or not.

****

After one week of talking to and seeing Deuce Jackson, Danica started walking around as if she were floating. She might as well have hung a balloon over her head that said, I am happy and in love. They spoke every day, and for the first time, he was meeting her for lunch. It was their first official dining date. They met at Aunt Florence's house on Wednesday, but Deuce could only spend an hour. He said it was an hour that was well worth it. Danica smiled to herself. She was doing that a lot lately.

Florence, who was on her way out, looked at her and shook her head. "Now, this is what I wanted to see."

Danica giggled girlishly. "Deuce is so sweet."

"And handsome and has a great bod'," Aunt Florence joked. "I have heard all the iterations of that statement lately."

Danica didn't want Deuce to leave when they first ate together. They found so many things to chat about. They had spent most of the next two days over the phone filling in the blanks about each other. They shouldn't still have so much to talk about, but they did. On Friday, they were supposed to have lunch at Deuce's workplace.

Danica couldn't recall feeling such anticipation for a weekend. They were going to go to church together, and she would hear him sing. She was outlining to Stella all the fun things that they were planning to do for the weekend and Stella was lapping up the latest development like it was an exotic romance story.

"Don't look now," Stella said, "but here comes the ex, and she's heading for us." Danica turned around and looked into the thunderous face of Kelsey Channer.

She had meant to ask Deuce about her. Kelsey was the girl who had broken his heart, and she was the reason why they were even talking and why Deuce joined Christian Singles.

Kelsey was married to Dale Julius. The three of them, Dale, Kelsey, and Deuce had a strange love triangle going on. Kelsey was a puzzle and an enigma.

Which woman in her right mind would leave Deuce for Dale? There wasn't even any comparison. Danica thought uncharitably. There was something about Dale that was just plain peculiar.

From the minute she met Dale, Danica knew something was off, her spirit of discernment had kicked in. Maybe Kelsey had no spirit of discernment.

Kelsey stopped at the table. "May I join you two for lunch?"

Danica looked at Stella.

Stella nodded. "Sure, Dr. Channer."

"Call me Kelsey." She sat down. She had a large salad on her plate. "I'm eating light today," she said casually. "I have a date with DJ tonight. Whenever we have our little dinner dates, I tend to eat a lot."

She then laughed shrilly in a completely fake and over the top way.

Danica cleared her throat. "I thought DJ had practice with his brothers tonight. We spoke just fifteen minutes ago, and he invited me to come along."

Kelsey looked at her, shocked. "So, it is true. You are trying to steal DJ from me!"

"I'm not trying to steal anyone," Danica hissed. "DJ and I have been talking for the past year and a half, and he has always been single. His ex-girlfriend married his friend, Dale Julius, the weasel, and left him brokenhearted."

"Yes, but he has forgiven me," Kelsey said, "and we're on the right track. I don't need you in our lives, creating havoc. Yes, I've messed up in the past," Kelsey said earnestly, "but I have learned from my mistakes. Haven't you ever made any mistakes?"

Danica looked at her face in astonishment. She hadn't expected this level of passion.

"I love DJ," Kelsey stressed every word. "and I will love him till the day I die. It took me too long to remember this, and he was going to forgive me this time around, I could feel it. And then here you are intruding in our lives."

"I am not intruding," Danica sputtered. "and I don't want to get into a catfight over DJ anyway, but let me tell you Kelsey, he was not going to go back to you whether I am in the picture or not. He has moved on."

"We'll see about that." Kelsey got up, grabbed her tray, and walked away.

"And suddenly, your life has become intriguing," Stella murmured. "I think she has a little crazy in her. I would tread carefully."

"I'll be fine," Danica said. "Don't doctors pledge to do no harm?"

"And yet, there are some that do." Stella intoned. "Be careful."

Chapter Eighteen

"**I** can't believe we're doing this," Deuce glance across at Danica. "I can't believe that you are here right now, and we're walking through the Blue Mountains."

"It's not exactly the Blue Mountains," Danica grinned. "It is glorious Holywell. Are you tired already, DJ?"

Deuce grinned. "No, I'm not."

"When I take my group here," Danica grinned. "I'm usually the one that is far ahead, and so I'm quite used to this pace."

"You are so cheeky," Deuce laughed. "Cut me some slack, you walk every day, I swim."

Danica grinned at him. She was almost sure she had stars in their eyes. She had never felt this happy. She was in the environment that she loved, hiking in the hills of Holywell with Deuce, a man she had gotten attached to. She glanced at him shyly.

"What?" he grinned.

"Nothing," Danica said. "I was just thinking how romantic this is, a picnic in the Holywell hills."

"Wait until we go to the Blue Mountains," Deuce grinned at her. "then you'll be saying it is more than romantic."

"I have never been there." Danica rubbed her hands together gleefully, "and I aim to enjoy every last bit of it. When are we going?" She was walking a little bit in front of Deuce, and she turned back and started walking backward.

"Say the word, Deuce Jackson, when are we going?"

Deuce grinned. "Your insatiable thirst for adventure has me scared; you know that?"

"Nah, it doesn't scare you. I think I know you by now," Danica said. "This is the sort of thing you love."

"Which makes us perfect for each other." Deuce winked at her. "I've never had a girlfriend who liked this amount of walking in the bushes."

"That's me," Danica nodded, her hair bounced up and down. "I love hiking gear more than formalwear."

"Chapstick to lipstick, picnics to fine dining," Deuce said, getting into the spirit of the bantering.

"Mountain hardware to Gucci," Danica grinned. "Can I play tennis with you and your brother?"

"Stop!" Deuce said. She was about to collide with a tree. Danica stopped and turned around.

"Oh DJ, you saved me,"

Deuce laughed. He walked up to her and held her hand. Danica gripped his hand in hers. "This feels right."

"It does," Deuce gazed at her.

"Tell me about Kelsey," Danica said. "Did it feel right with her too?"

Deuce squeeze her fingers tighter and sighed. "At one time, Yes."

"Did you have dinner with her the other day and gave her

false hope that you guys will get back together?" Danica asked seriously.

Deuce stopped. "I had dinner with her, but I gave her no hope that we will get back together. At the back of my thoughts, I might have felt a little vulnerable. I have told myself that Kelsey was 'the one', and no one could replace her, but I've come to realize that that is not true. The past year with you helped me to forget her, and when she came back, I didn't feel the way I used to."

Danica beamed at him; a beatific smile crossed her face. "I am so grateful we ran into each other, DJ."

"No Missy," DJ leaned closer to her. "I came and found you. When I saw you, it was instant for me, you know. I was like, Who's that girl?"

"So, you're into me?" Danica asked coyly.

"Oh, yes." Deuce nodded, "so into you that you wouldn't believe. This past week I've been counting my blessings, you know. I think you're a blessing. And I memorized your phone number. I will never forget it unless I'm brain damaged."

Danica laughed. "And I'll never forget yours."

They stopped under a giant cotton tree.

"Now, this looks like it has been here since the beginning of time," Danica whispered, "crafted by a God who pays minute attention to details. Look at the bark of this thing," she whispered in awe.

She turned to Deuce, but he wasn't looking at the tree bark. He was looking at her.

"I do marvel at a God who can create such exquisite beauty." He smiled at her.

Danica smiled. "I think that there are things that are orchestrated, and me finding you was arranged somehow. You remember the story of Abraham and Sarah? I think it was the first time when he tried to, to pass off Sarah as his sister, to Pharaoh. The Pharaoh got a dream in which God told him, 'don't you dare touch that woman'."

Deuce nodded.

"God was working on their relationship," Danica said with certainty. "He was intervening on behalf of Abraham. It's amazing. If you think about it."

"It is amazing." Deuce nodded.

"So that's why I think Dale Julius would not have gotten far with me," Danica said. "When I asked God to take care of my day and my life, and that I'm trusting him, I have no doubt that he is taking care of all of the little machinations that goes on around me. I've always said being a Christian is a superpower. You have silent beings following you around and helping you navigate all the bad things. The amazing thing is you can't see it, but it's happening."

Deuce looked at her transfixed. "I love to hear a godly woman speak. He walked closer to her and kissed her on the lips—just a brief hard kiss. Danica looked at him wide-eyed and then cleared her throat.

"I was going to say something else just as profound, but I just can't remember."

"You were going to say," Deuce said, "That you are happy that I'm in your life and that God has put us together for a reason."

"That must be it." Danica reached up to kiss him this time.

****

"I am really happy, Aunt Florence," Danica said, running around the kitchen. "I'm so happy I didn't bother getting up to go walking this morning. And I'm late for work."

Florence chuckled. "I was talking to Celia before you came in last night..."

Danica glanced at her aunt. "You mean Deuce's mom?"

"One and the same," Florence said, "and we were speculating whether we should be planning two weddings this year. Ace has all but hinted that he is so into Kiya that there will be no one else for him, and you and Deuce seem like you're on that track."

Danica grinned. "I wouldn't say no if he proposed today."

Florence smiled widely. "That's my girl. You know what you want, and you're not beating around the bush, and I can vouch for Deuce. You see, I personally know that he's a forever kind of man—the things that Kelsey put him through, and he still stayed faithful to her."

Danica scolded. "I don't want to talk about Kelsey."

"Neither does Celia," Florence said. "She was quite excited to talk about you though. She's coming up tomorrow for a girls only lunch. Can you make it, or are you taking your group somewhere?"

"No, I'll make it," Danica said. "We have quite a few places that we will want to go. However, I'll have to spend the rest of this week along with HR finding someone to replace Opal."

"I don't understand Opal, I liked her, but she was so rude to me, I wonder who else got that attitude." Florence snorted.

"I know," Danica said. " She's coming to pick up her things today, and I'm not looking forward to the confrontation."

"Be careful," Florence said.

"I always am." Danica headed to the door. When she opened the front door, she saw a bouquet with a note attached to it.

These flowers were not the roses that Dale Julius used to send. These were the black-eyed Susans that grew wild in front of the admin office. They were tied together in a neat little bundle. Danica picked it up apprehensively and read the note.

'I am better than him. Give me a chance, Dale Julius'.

"What's keeping you?" Florence asked from behind her.

"He just won't go away," Danica said to her aunt. "Do you think he's dangerous?"

"Let me see that," Florence took the note and looked at it.

"He probably spent the weekend with his mother and is watching us," Danica said.

"Well, this is not necessarily dangerous," Florence said reluctantly, "but I am going to talk with his mother. Maybe she can tell him to stop stalking you. This feels stalkerish, doesn't it?"

"That's the word," Danica said. "That is it. He's stalking me."

"I'll speak to Leona Julius. I don't want you to feel uncomfortable here and when he stays on the weekend, it's too close for comfort. He needs to move on like a normal person," Florence muttered.

Danica left the house, but not before looking around to see if Dale's car was in his mother's driveway. He wasn't there, but he had been there sometime today. While she was telling herself not to overreact, she couldn't shake an uncomfortable feeling about this whole Dale Julius thing.

It was the same thing on Tuesday morning. A bundle of Black-eyed Susan plants with a little tie around them and a note was left at her doorstep at the staff quarters.

She was heading for work when she saw it. The note read. 'If I can't have you, he won't either.' This one scared her.

She immediately took the note to Quade's office. She almost regretted it. When she walked into Quade's outer office, she saw Kelsey Channer sitting there looking pretty.

Kelsey looked up when she entered the office area and then looked at her Black-eyed Susans and snickered.

"Wildflowers! I thought Deuce had more taste than that."

"I got these from your kooky ex-husband," Danica grunted. "First he tried pretending that he was DJ. And now he is stalking me, and I don't like it. This note says, *if I can't have you, he won't either.*"

"Dale has always been weird. Come to think of it, you are a little weird too," Kelsey said. "Maybe you should stop seeing Deuce and date Dale, all of this would go away."

"You would like that, wouldn't you," Danica huffed.

"I'd love it," Kelsey said.

Danica didn't bother sitting in the office to wait for Quade. She would be back later. Maybe she was making a big deal of nothing.

She dumped the flowers and the note on her way out. She would have to speak to Leona Julius herself. Aunt Florence had not gotten through to that woman.

****

"Tell your son to stop stalking me." Danica didn't mince words when she saw Leona Julius in the lobby area when she was heading for lunch.

Leona gasped. "Miss Hunt, those spurious allegations are absurd. My son is not a stalker."

"So why is he leaving messages under my door?" Danica asked.

"I have no explanation as to why he is fixated on you but that is not stalking. He seems to think that you led him on."

"Me?" Danica widened her eyes. "He pretended to be someone else. I thought he was the man I was talking to for a year and a half. It turns out he was not. It was too easy for him to lie to me, so I don't trust him!"

Leona grimaced. "I heard about the whole sordid affair, and I must say, his behavior was surprising."

Danica's anger subsided; Leona looked crestfallen.

"All my children have issues." She said it without any self-pity, just a matter of fact voice. "I'll do my best to fix this." She nodded at Danica and then headed toward the arts and crafts area.

Danica watched her leave and wondered how she was going to fix it. Why was it that the one time in her life when things were going so well, there had to be somebody to rain on her parade.

Chapter Nineteen

Deuce hung up the phone from a call with Danica. She had just told him about the 'notes' from Dale Julius. It was lunchtime, and he had a break, so he headed straight for Dale's office. Dale was standing in the lobby with a gentleman he assumed was a patient.

Deuce glared at him. "I need to talk to you."

Dale had on one of those fixed smiles on his face. Deuce didn't trust that smile; he had never trusted that smile. Dale walked over to him as if they were on the best of terms.

"Your teeth look perfectly aligned," Dale said. "I assume you wore braces when you were twelve or so?"

"I'm not here to talk about my teeth." Deuce looked at him in astonishment. "Are you totally off your rockers? Stop leaving notes for Danica!"

"So, she's your girlfriend now?" Dale asked the smile slipped from his face. "You weren't joking when you said that you two told each other everything, were you? I was just testing the theory."

"You have an explanation for everything, don't you?" Deuce looked at him. "You just happened to find my phone, you just happened to send text messages on my behalf, and now you just happen to send notes to her to test whether she's my girlfriend or not? Are we in fifth grade? How gullible do you think I am? Stop sending her notes. It is scaring her."

"What is it about you that's so appealing?" Dale asked almost contemplatively. "Why you? She met me face to face first."

"Because you are phony, and she could sense it!" Deuce glared at him. "People, in general, don't like pathological liars."

"And there I was, thinking that we could be friends again," Dale said. "There was a time when I used to fantasize that we were brothers."

"We'll never be friends again," Deuce said to him. "I think that ship has sailed with your recent behavior."

"That's fine." Dale shrugged. "I will survive. You sound just like Kelsey; she said the same thing to me, we will never be friends again, as if I would want to be friends with her. I have an idea, why don't you two hook up again and leave Danica to me?"

Dale's phony smile was back.

"No," Deuce glared at him. "I have a better idea, why don't you go back to Kelsey and leave Danica alone. It seems as if you want everybody that I want or have ever been with."

"I don't know about that," Dale said, "Danica has made me hopeful again, she is a wonderful girl, and I don't see why I should step back just because you decided that you wanted her for yourself."

Deuce sighed. " If you continue this way, we'll just have to get the police involved."

"And tell the police what?" Dale asked. "I have done nothing but leave her a couple flowers and a friendly notes. As I see it, you're making more of this than there is because you are trying to get rid of the competition. All is fair in love and war."

Deuce slammed out of the office in disbelief. This guy was quoting English proverbs, 'All is fair in love and war.' He didn't see anything wrong with his current behavior. It was baffling to him, but he wouldn't let Dale's strange fascination with Danica derail his relationship with her.

They were working up to something solid and real. He knew it in his head, he felt it in his heart, and he wasn't going to step back and allow Dale to dictate where they went with their relationship.

They had one week of respite from both Dale and Kelsey, but Deuce was amazed that Kelsey had given up. He was even more amazed that Dale Julius had backed off after declaring that all was fair in love and war.

Deuce and Danica hiked, and they went to dinners. The first time that Danica came to his apartment, she declared that he needed houseplants. The second time she carried two peace lilies. Everything was going swimmingly.

They were building a real relationship, but then Kelsey started calling. Usually, at about one o'clock in the morning.

"Deuce, I can't live without you."

"You can, and you have," Deuce said. "Kelsey, what's going on with you?"

"I made a vow to leave you alone," Kelsey said, "I really did. And I was becoming successful at it, and then today I saw your little miss Danica. You know, that's not her natural hair color, don't you? She has in box color number forty-eight, honey brown. I'm telling you, DJ, if a woman lies about her hair, she can lie about anything."

Deuce laughed. "Kelsey, it's one o'clock in the morning. I'm not discussing Danica's hair with you."

"I hate her!" Kelsey sobbed down the phone.

"You are acting crazy," Deuce said. "have you been drinking?"

Kelsey hung up on him, and he thought that would have been the end of it, but she called him the next night, and the night after that, and the night after that. It took him a week before he started putting his phone on silent. She started leaving him long teary messages about how sorry she was and how unforgiving he was when he no longer took her calls.

One night he answered the phone, mainly because he was on his way home from a date with Danica. He was racking up mileage from his frequent visits to Golden Acres.

"For the purposes of your romance," Quade had told him earlier, "you should just come and stay with me. I have room."

Deuce was almost considering it. What he wanted more than anything was to be with Danica every day and night. Marriage was on his brain, and he didn't want to fool around with this relationship. And so he answered the phone tersely, maybe a bit too tersely.

"Kelsey, you are a grown woman, a doctor with a terminal degree. Have you stopped visiting your therapist?"

"No," Kelsey said snappily. "You are our main topic of conversation these days. You and your stubbornness." Her voice softened somewhat. "If you didn't have Danica distracting you, we would be back together by now."

"I doubt it," Deuce said. "Kelsey, give it up."

She hung up the phone on him again.

*****

Deuce called Danica as soon as he reached home, she always insisted on it.

"I feel guilty about you coming up here early tomorrow morning," Danica said. "You just got home. You'll probably only get five hours of sleep."

Deuce laughed. "I'll be fine. I've gotten by on less sleep."

"But we're going walking up the Blue Mountain, and it's not a light trek."

"But you'll be carrying ten senior citizens with you. Isn't that true?" Deuce said. "If they keep up better than me, then I know I'm really out of shape."

Danica chuckled. "We'll see how it goes. The oldest person coming on the tour is eighty-six, and I think he's also the spriteliest."

"I hope I can keep up with Mr. Peterson," Deuce chuckled. "See you tomorrow, Princess."

"Sweet dreams," Danica said huskily.

Deuce set his alarm. He was tempted to ignore it when it went off at 5:30, but he remembered that he was going to see Danica soon and he jumped up out of bed.

They would spend the entire day together, chaperoned by ten elderly busybodies, but that wasn't daunting.

Usually, he would spend his Ash Wednesdays in bed, grateful for a lazy day but not today. He laced up his hiking boots, checked the inventory in his hiking bag, and called Danica. He wanted to tease her and ask her if she was up.

Her phone rang without an answer several times. After the fifth time dialing her number, he began to worry. What if she wasn't awake? He was five minutes from Golden Acres when he tried again. When Quade answered, he knew something was wrong.

"What's wrong?" He asked, trying not to panic.

"That's what we want to know," Quade said. "We found her hiking bag and her phone in the parking lot. We're scoring the whole place for her; security is bringing up the footage now."

Deuce didn't know what to think. He felt raw, unfettered panic coursing through him. His hand trembled on the steering wheel.

"Dear God, keep her safe," he whispered.

What else could he do? He had to take comfort in the fact that Danica knew she had superpowers, invisible guardian angels.

But where was she?

Chapter Twenty

When Deuce arrived at Golden Acres, he saw a heavy security presence throughout the grounds.

They gave him a hard time at the gate, but he endured the rigor of their scrutiny. The day had moved from foggy dark to a dull grey with the sun in the distance and it started drizzling. Some residents were looming around the admin building, and Quade was in the lobby area on his phone. When he saw Deuce, he waved.

"I can't believe this is happening," Quade said. "We have cameras all around and security presence on the grounds. How could Danica just disappear?"

"That's my question," Deuce pushed his hands in his jacket pocket to warm them up, they were feeling cold and trembly. "We were going to hang out together today, and we were excited about it."

"This is beyond comprehension," Quade murmured. "I was headed to the security section; do you want to come?"

Deuce nodded.

"I'm so sorry about this," Quade sighed. "So sorry."

"It's not your fault," Deuce looked at the big clock in the lobby area, it was ten minutes after six.

"This had to be an inside job, somebody who is familiar with our security procedures," Quade muttered as if he was talking to himself.

Deuce didn't even want to think about what this would mean. He was still holding out hope that Danica had voluntarily gone off somewhere.

He didn't want the thoughts in his head to let loose. He didn't want to take them out, dust them off and start panicking.

They entered the section where the security personnel were located. There were banks of monitors all around, surveying different sections of the property. Quade introduced Deuce to Leonard, the head of security.

He had on a bold Golden Acres Security t-shirt.

"Leonard and his team were trained by Wiley Securities," Quade said. "They are the best in the business."

"Okay, so this is what we found," Leonard said briskly. He pointed to the main monitor that he and two other guys were hovering over.

Deuce looked at the footage. It was a view of the parking lot.

Danica approached her car with a hiking bag in hand. She left the bag on the car bonnet, opened the door, and was rummaging around in there. While she was doing so, a silver car drove up. It had heavily tinted windows.

What looked like an elderly man came out of the backseat, he said something to Danica, she closed her car door and headed for the backseat of his car. He was pointing to something in the back.

It was too dark to see what it was on the camera, but it was evident that Danica leaned down, as if she was looking at something and the old man casually pushed her into the car and got in after her, and the car spun around and left the parking lot.

"There were three people in the car when they checked in," Leonard said. "There was a young couple who identified themselves as Bella and David Morgan. They claimed that they live in the community.

"Their father, Ken Morgan, was going on the Blue Mountains with Danica. The name was on the list, so the security officer at the front gate let them in. It was supposed to be a simple drop off."

Quade sighed. "This does not look good. We should call the police."

"Way ahead of you on that one," Leonard said. "I already called Saint Wiley, who has contacts all over the police force."

"Who would do this?" Quade looked at Deuce.

Deuce inhaled raggedly. "Well, Kelsey and Dale Julius come to mind."

Leonard looked between him and Quade.

"Dale Julius, the doctor?" Leonard asked. "Leona Julius' son?"

Deuce nodded.

"Who is Kelsey?"

"She's a doctor on our staff. She works here on Mondays and Wednesdays," Quade added.

"I'll have our investigators check out Dr. Kelsey and Dr. Dale," Leonard said. "What's the motive, though?"

"Yes." Quade looked at Deuce confusion in his eyes. "What on earth is going on? At first, I thought that girl that we let go, may be involved, Opal. She didn't like getting fired. She thought that we were biased because she was here longer than Danica, but she was rude to Aunt Florence, and she wanted Opal gone."

"I will check her out too." Leonard picked up his cellphone and waited for whoever was on the other end to pick up.

Quade started pacing. "We can't alarm the residents. Some of them are already in the lobby area, waiting for Danica. I'll have to tell them that the trip is canceled."

Deuce was watching them, a sense of incredulity encasing him. He sat on one of the chairs in a daze.

"Why would you think Dale or Kelsey?" Quade stopped pacing. "You never answered."

"Dale was sending her notes. He said stuff like if she doesn't choose him, neither of us will have her."

Deuce said faintly, "I didn't think they were harmless, so I spoke to him, and he backed off."

Quade widened his eyes.

"What!" Leonard was half listening while on the phone.

"And Kelsey calls me in the wee hours of the morning and says stuff about Danica," Deuce added with a sigh. "The last time she declared that Danica would never love me as she did."

"All of this drama in my backyard," Quade muttered, "and now Danica is missing."

"Are any of these people capable of doing bad things, Deuce?"

Deuce held his head in his hand. "You never really know people, do you? What can I say? I have no idea."

"I'm getting right on this. I am calling in Wiley Security," Leonard said. "They work faster than the police."

Quade patted Deuce on his shoulder. "We are not going to panic. Let's hope she is safe."

Deuce clenched his fist convulsively. "Please God, let it

be so."

****

Danica woke up, and her head was pounding. She was in a car, and she was lying on someone's lap. She struggled to open her eyes and tried to move her head, but she felt paralyzed. She couldn't feel her hands and she couldn't feel her feet. Memories of her near brush with rape came flashing through her mind.

"No!" she struggled to speak, but her tongue was not cooperating. She made a gargled sound. That didn't even sound human.

"Don't move," a gravelly voice said over her head. "You'll get over it slowly."

"Who are you?" Danica croaked. Her tongue was finally working. "Where are you taking me?"

"I am taking you somewhere safe. They will never hurt you again." The man reassured her.

"Are you crazy?" Danica struggled to move. "I wasn't unsafe."

"Some people don't know what's good for them," the lady in the front said. "Give her another dose to calm her down. That dose wore off too fast, and we have another couple of hours to go."

"I have to be careful with this." The man grunted. "It's a liquid tranquilizer. It can kill her. The doctor doesn't want her dead. She said I should use this with caution."

"Which Doctor?" Danica asked. "What is going on?"

The old man covered her face with another rag.

Chapter Twenty-One

Deuce felt as if he was in a state of suspended animation. It was the longest, hellish three days of his life.

Everyone around him was moving, but he was frozen in a petrified, inanimate state. He had canceled all his appointments for the rest of the week and had basically camped out at his Aunt Florence's house, waiting for news.

Danica's parents had arrived on the island the day before. He met her mother, Sarah, and her father, Jim. They were staying with Florence as well. They had all bonded in mutual terror. Deuce was afraid to go home.

He didn't want to be alone with his thoughts and to feel frightened by the possibility that something could be wrong with Danica. He was quite fine staying with Florence, where it seemed dozens of persons kept going in and out of the house.

Danica had a huge family. They descended on Golden Acres in fits and spurts. Sometimes there were up to ten or twelve people in the living room.

Danica's grandmother, Heather Greyson, came with her security team, and they interviewed and re-interviewed the same people that Wiley Securities did, and they sat and compared notes.

By now, all the residents knew what happened and were suitably alarmed. There was so much tension in the air; it could be sliced with a knife.

Deuce was tired of it. His neck had a constant pain that he knew was caused by the tension of it all. He took a walk along the regular hiking trail, and he passed Leona Julius on the way.

She had binoculars around her neck.

"Good morning." Deuce murmured when she passed him.

She stopped. "Have they found her yet?"

"No!" Deuce growled. Obviously, she was not 'found'. He hated how she said, found.

Found implied something that he was not even going to consider. He preferred to think of her as coming back, not being found.

"No need to sound so testy, young man," Leona said, "I just asked a question."

"I'm sorry," Deuce said. "She means a lot to me; I just wish we had met sooner. I had her for a month, and now she is gone."

"The police questioned Dale, you know." Leona sniffed. "It was so degrading to even think that my Dale would have anything to do with this. He was a bit obsessed with her, but to imply he'd have anything to do with this is crazy."

"Dale is the one who is crazy," Deuce said. "He wrote her notes saying all different kinds of weird creepy stuff. He was the first person I suspected when Danica went missing. I was the one who gave the police his name."

"And to think he considers you his friend," Leona huffed. "You should know better than anyone that Dale is not capable of anything like this. That private investigation firm even checked his phone records. That's an invasion of privacy."

Deuce sighed. "But it cleared him, didn't it? And if you were honest, you would admit that he was acting a bit unhinged."

"I have three children," Leona said, "and he's the last good one left... I will admit nothing."

Deuce didn't even bother commenting.

"Excuse me." Deuce walked past Leona and headed for the security offices. Saint Wiley was at the front, staring down at the parking lot. Deuce was standing beside him.

"How are you holding up?" Saint asked him.

"Barely," Deuce said. "Is there anything new?"

"Nothing," Saint said. "It's as if she vanished into thin air. That car is nowhere to be found. The car was registered to someone who is no longer alive. It was a well-planned kidnapping," Saint sighed, "but this is my specialty. I do get down to the nitty-gritty of mysteries. Don't worry, Deuce; we'll find your girl."

"What about Kelsey?" Deuce asked. "Do you think she had anything to do with it?"

"Kelsey Channer," Saint shook his head. "She's something else, isn't she? We interviewed her twice, and we are almost sure that she had nothing to do with this."

"You pulled her phone records like you did Dale's?" Deuce asked.

"Yup," Saint said, "and there are quite a number of calls to you. I can see why you thought she would be a suspect. However, she had an alibi for the night and the morning, she was at Sunrise Medical, we even have footage of her, and all of her calls checked out."

Deuce inhaled and then exhaled loudly. "So who could it be? I'm at my wit's end. Everybody liked Danica."

"I know how you feel," Saint said. "But don't worry, just pray."

His phone rang, and he took the phone call.

Deuce walked down to the parking lot, still looking around for clues. Maybe there was something all of them were missing.

The anxiety and stress were eating at him.

He was so focused on his inner thoughts; he didn't even hear when Kelsey drove up. She slammed the car door and was right in front of him before he saw her.

"I have clinic today," Kelsey said before he could even ask her why she was there. "I work here, you know, and I didn't do this."

"Are you sure, Kelsey?" Deuce asked.

"Of course, I'm sure," Kelsey widened her eyes. "I can't even believe you would think I would do this. You feel for this girl, don't you?"

"I do love her," Deuce said. "It's nothing like what I had with you. With Danica, things just feel right."

"Right," Kelsey swallowed. "Well, I hope she comes back to you alive and safe. And though this pains me to say, I apologize for being a jerk these last couple of weeks and saying bad things about Danica.

"I have got to stop drunk dialing you. I didn't mean any of the bad things I may have said about Danica. I guess I just have to accept that you have moved on and I should move on too."

Deuce nodded and watched as Kelsey walked away. He didn't know if he should believe her. He didn't trust anyone right now.

****

Danica slipped in and out of consciousness.

She concluded after waking up the first time that she was in a dorm of some sort. They were bunk beds all around, and several women came in and out of the room. They were dressed strangely in shapeless robe-like dresses. Most of them were in a drab beige color. The women all had on headwear too, the same color as the clothes.

One of them, an older looking lady, sat with her constantly through every waking moment. She had seen the drab colors and the robe-like beige dress before. It was on Grace, the girl who had stowed away on the tour bus.

"Where am I?" she asked on the third day.

"Oh, you are awake," the lady said softly. Thank God, Rufus went a bit heavy with the tranquilizer, he double dosed you. I told him to be careful.

"Where is this?" Danica tried to raise her head from the pillow.

"We are in the compound of Machseh, a place of refuge."

"Huh?" Danica looked at the woman. She could be anywhere in her thirties or forties; her skin was smooth and unlined, and she was quite pretty. Her eyes were hazel, and they seemed to dominate her face.

"Machseh means refuge in Hebrew," the lady explained. "We rescued you from a very bad situation."

"Rescued me?" Danica opened her mouth, "but I didn't need rescuing."

"Everyone in the world outside needs rescuing. You will come to love it here." She smiled. "We live a simple life. We grow our own food without fertilizers and pesticides, we have a fresh source of water from a well that has the purest water you will ever taste, our source is from the hills, no one lives up there, and best of all we have a tight-knit community that loves others."

"What is this, some kind of cult?" Danica asked hoarsely.

"We do not like the word cult." The lady tightened her lips in disapproval. "We are families that come together to wait on the end of days and to disassociate ourselves from the materialistic world."

Danica widened her eyes. "But I don't want to disassociate myself. I want to take my clients on a Blue Mountain hike and spend some time with my boyfriend. I'm here against my will."

"Shhh." The lady gasped. "You must not speak like this. I cannot afford for Brother Cyrus to hear you say that. We spent resources to get you here, and up here you will stay."

"Who is brother Cyrus and who are you?"

"My Hebrew name is Azaria; it means God has helped. I only use that name now, and Brother Cyrus is the head of the flock. I told him about your dire situation, and that is why we rescued you."

"You mean you kidnapped me!" Danica raised her hand looked around. Her hair felt matted, and her mouth felt dry.

"We're not in the business of kidnapping," Azaria said disapprovingly. "And please do not say that word around here. We do not want the government's scrutiny. Come, now that you are well, you can have a bath, and I can give you something to eat. We're not prisoners. You will get acclimatized to here soon enough." Azaria smiled at her. "Julie will give you a change of garment, and then she'll show you around."

Azaria got up and left a confused Danica, staring at her retreating back in panic.

Chapter Twenty-Two

The beige dresses were heavy and felt rough to the touch, but Danica was thankful for it because the water had been ice cold, and she had been forced to wash her hair. Julie handed her a sandal and a thong to pull back her hair.

"We make our own soap and slippers," Julie said helpfully. "Did you like the scent of the soap you used?"

"It was nice," Danica said grudgingly. "What was it?"

"Jasmine. It boosts energy." Julie said happily. "Doctor Azaria said I should give it to you to wake up your skin and make you feel refreshed you had a rough couple of days. We were wondering if you were going to wake up fully."

"Doctor Azaria? She's a doctor?" Danica asked.

"One of the best herbal doctors around," Julie said happily. "She even helps outsiders."

"So you guys are quite self-sufficient," Danica said.

"Oh yes," Julie nodded. "Brother Cyrus even has some of us making paper from banana bark."

"Interesting," Danica said, looking around. She had bathed in a big bathroom that reminded her of her time on a college dorm. There was a large room with bunk beds.

"The single women and children sleep here," Julie offered. She was friendly enough. "You'll love it up here," Julie added.

"What is this place?" Danica asked. "I don't get it. Can you leave if you want?"

"Nobody wants to leave." Julie looked at her as if she was crazy. "Brother Cyrus started this as a place of refuge for people who need help."

"But I don't need any help," Danica said.

"But you had to have needed help," Julie insisted, "or else Doctor Azaria would not have had you taken up here. I heard you came from Kingston. How is it there?"

"Lovely," Danica said sarcastically. "How can I speak to this Brother Cyrus?"

They exited the dorm house, and Danica realized that they were in a village. The buildings were modern enough. It reminded her of a movie set she had toured at Universal Studios. There were several shops to the left and the right, and there was a church in the distance, on the hillside, and a paved road about a mile long.

Julie started speaking. "This is the village. We make most of our things here. There is the farm," she pointed to the left.

It was a large farm that went as far as Danica could see.

"There is the orchard." Julie pointed to the right. In that direction, there was a neat row of houses.

"Brother Cyrus owned the land up here," Julie said. "And he created a place for us all to be safe. That is where Brother Cyrus' office is," Julie whispered reverently.

Danica imagined brother Cyrus to be a wizened old man, and she was hoping that she could appeal to his common sense. She was kidnapped, but she didn't know by whom and she didn't know why.

"I want to see him," Danica said.

"No," Julie shook her head. "Women are not supposed to go into his office, his sacred space."

Danica widened her eyes. *What in the nineteenth century is going on up here?* Brother Cyrus sounded like he was running a different sort of culture.

"A woman should be seen and not heard, that is what this is." Danica snorted.

Julie looked confused at the disdain she saw in her face. "What is wrong with that? Men are our superiors in every way."

Danica swallowed her initial retort; it would not be complimentary to Brother Cyrus. "But we are created equal. We were supposed to be partners."

Julie looked shocked at the concept.

"Reread the Biblical account and tell that to your Brother Cyrus next time," Danica muttered. She looked around for a way to escape. She could see a big metal gate at the bottom of the hill. Beyond that was greenery, no buildings, no movement. It was as if they were in the middle of nowhere. There had to be some way out of here.

"Which parish is this?" She asked Julie.

"Trelawny," Julie said.

"Is this close to Crimson Hill?" Danica asked.

"It's another hill over," Julie said, looking at her. "You can't leave here, you know," Julie said. "A few persons have tried."

"But if it's so great," Danica said, "Why did they try to leave?"

Julie moved closer to her and then looked around. "There are some persons who think the outside world is better than here."

Danica nodded. "I think so too."

"It can't be better," Julie said. "There is crime out there and violence and immorality of all kinds. It's better here."

"How old are you?" Danica asked.

"Sixteen," Julie said, "and I have lived here six years."

"When my mother moved here, we were on the run from my father. Brother Cyrus took us in and treated us right, so my mother said she will never leave."

Danica looked around again for an escape route. She wasn't going to stay here. She didn't care if it was a place of refuge for some people. It wasn't a place of refuge for her. She wanted to go home. She missed Deuce, and everybody else must be worried sick about her.

Two men passed by her in the same robe and sandals. She felt as if she was in a Bible play.

"I want to go home," she said to Julie. "Please, just help me."

Julie shook her head. "You can't. You should be hungry. Let's go."

She was hungry, and for her to escape, she needed some food in her. They went to a building that she quickly realized was the cafeteria. Azaria met them at the door.

"What took so long, Julie?"

"I was just showing her around," Julie said, "Come with me," Azaria said, "Brother Cyrus wants to meet you."

Julie melted into the crowd. There was a line at the food counter, and Danica had to admit that the food smelled good. She suddenly felt faint with hunger. Azaria led her over to a table where a surprisingly handsome man was sitting. He was probably in his late 30s or early 40s.

This couldn't be Brother Cyrus?

Azaria hung her head demurely when they reached the

table. So Danica assumed it was.

"Have a seat Danica," he said. His voice was like warm honey.

Danica was fascinated with him despite herself.

"I am Cyrus," he said. Danica sat down and was promptly served porridge, pineapple, and orange juice.

"I heard you were out for three days," Cyrus said in that same smooth voice. "You must be hungry, please eat. We will speak after."

Danica didn't need to be told twice. She had never tasted pineapple so sweet as the one that she sunk her teeth into, nor had she ever had porridge so creamy and rich. She didn't even think if it had in milk, she just gobbled it down like a starving person. Cyrus looked at her as she slowly went through all of the food.

He and Danica were the only ones that were served. Everyone else had to join the line to get their breakfast.

"So," Cyrus said when she had finished eating, "I hear you have been running away from an abusive relationship."

"No," Danica said, "That's not true."

Cyrus looked at her. "You are a pretty girl."

"Thank you," Danica said.

"I could make you my fifth wife. I don't abuse women."

"I already have a boyfriend," Danica said, "his name is Deuce Jackson. I was going to have a Blue Mountain tour with my clients when I was kidnapped. This is not right. I want to go home."

"Deuce Jackson?" Cyrus frowned. "He is a children's doctor?"

"Yes," Danica nodded. "Do you know him?"

Cyrus didn't answer. He leaned back in his chair. "This is quite the conundrum, Danica. We help people, and you do not seem as if you need the help."

"That's right." That's what I've been trying to tell Azaria and that girl, Julie. My family will be looking for me."

"Family?" Cyrus raised an eyebrow.

"Do you know, the Wiley supermarkets?" Danica said earnestly. "The owners are my cousins. Greyson Industries? The owner married my grandmother. My cousin Saint Wiley has a security company, and he probably has all his men out right now. My parents will pay whatever reward it is that you want. I am their only child."

Cyrus opened his mouth in shock.

"My cousins, Giselle, Tiana and Elsa, their brother is Senator Toddy Pryce! I can't imagine that they'll just sit idly by while I'm missing. "

Cyrus clapped his hands once, and it made Danica jump. She stopped talking and watched to see what was happening.

The entire place stilled and all the buzzing in the cafeteria stopped.

"Azaria Julius," Cyrus growled. Azaria, who had been standing in the line, looked over at them guiltily. "You have brought trouble upon us, Azaria." Cyrus got up. "Follow me." He indicated to Danica.

Danica got up hurriedly.

"You too, Azaria," he said, heading through the door.

Chapter Twenty-Three

Deuce had abandoned his vigil in the security section and was sitting in the conference room with Quade and Ace. They were looking at the same video that showed when Danica was taken from the parking lot.

Quade had the video frozen on the old man's face. It was the clearest picture that they had. Ace was drumming his fingers on the table, and Quade was twiddling his thumbs. They could hear the cleaning crew going through the offices. One of them, a pretty young lady, with a cut that looked to be healing on her forehead, came through the door.

"Oh, I'm sorry," she said. "I didn't know anyone was in there. I was supposed to be cleaning the conference room."

Quade looked at her. "You can clean around us, Grace." She came further into the room and looked at the screen. And then she stopped.

"That's Brother Samuel."

"You know this guy?" both Quade and Ace asked at the

same time.

Grace swallowed. "Yes. Were they up here looking for me? I thought up here was the safest place to go without them finding me."

"No," Quade said, "that is the man that took Danica."

"They took Miss Danica?" Grace shook her head. "Why?"

"Who are they?" Deuce asked.

"They are the Machseh people. They rescue people from the sins of this world." Grace snared. "But some of them are greater sinners than the people out here, if you asked me. They beat people for every little thing, and they starve people until they are willing to agree to anything."

Grace was in full flow. "They marry the girls to the men in the compound as soon as they hit puberty. Danica is pretty. She's probably married to Brother Cyrus by now."

Deuce stood up before she stopped speaking. "Where are these Machseh people?"

"In the Trelawny Hills," Grace said. "I can give you directions, but I'm not going anywhere near there again."

*****

Three helicopters filled with police, soldiers, and Saint Wiley's security personnel landed in the middle of the Machseh property. It took them nearly an hour to reach there and five minutes to walk through the fields to the main compound.

A lone man in a beige robe greeted them. Deuce was glad he had insisted on coming with Saint.

"This is private property gentlemen, and we are a non-violent people living our lives peacefully," the man said, holding up both hands.

"Where is Danica?" Deuce asked, not mincing words.

"She left of her own free will," the man spoke slowly and deliberately. "We sent her off a mere twenty minutes ago."

"Sent her off to where?" Deuce asked.

"She walked through the gate of her own free will," Cyrus said.

"But why on earth did you kidnap her?" Deuce asked.

"We do not kidnap people," Cyrus said without an expression on his face. "Could your men lower their guns?"

Saint made the sign for them to lower their guns, and they did.

"Thank you," Cyrus said. "Unbeknownst to me, one Azaria Julius was contacted by her mother, Leona Julius. She was told by Leona that there is a woman named Danica, who needed our help."

"Leona," Deuce gritted his teeth.

"We rescue people from time to time," Cyrus said benignly. "And Azaria thought that this case was very dire, her mother described it as such."

"Her mother is a liar!" Deuce said.

"That is what we found out," Cyrus said, "and as soon as I found out, I told Danica that she was free to go. We are not in the business of keeping prisoners."

"So why was it necessary to kidnap her?" Saint was the one who asked.

"I had no idea she was taken against her will," Cyrus said. "I thought she came of her own free will. I consented to send my people on a rescue mission. We do that from time to time; it is necessary to do so in some cases usually in cases of abuse, we are a safe haven."

"Which direction did she go?" Deuce said. "The least you could do is allow her to call somebody or take her back."

Cyrus nodded. "I take your point, but the lady was quite eager to leave, she said she didn't need any further help from us. She went in that direction." Cyrus pointed to the gate.

"We could find her easier by air," Saint suggested.

"It's okay. I'll get her." Deuce walked toward the gate. Danica was a fit woman who could cover much distance in fifteen minutes, so he was surprised that he didn't have to walk long.

It took him five minutes to find her. She was sitting at the side of the road; she was scratching herself in frantic motions. Her face was red and blotchy, and one of her eyes was almost swollen shut.

"My goodness!" Deuce gasped out loud, "what have they done to you?"

Danica whipped her head around. "DJ! Am I hallucinating? I just asked God to rescue me! He is an on-time God."

Deuce chuckled. "Yes, I am real."

"I have an allergy." Danica got up, "I think there was milk in some porridge I had today. It was so creamy and good I didn't even care when I scarfed it down."

She started scratching her stomach, pulling up her blouse to reveal the beginnings of a scary-looking rash which was coming from her neck. "My skin is crawling all over."

Deuce watched her with a smile on his face. "You look awful, and I have never been so happy to see you."

"Help me scratch," Danica said, coming over to him.

Deuce gathered her in his arms and put his hand on her naked back. "Somehow, I never thought that our first time so close would be a scratching session."

Danica laughed. "I can't believe you are seeing me like this with welts all over my face and neck. I must look like a hot mess."

"I don't care." Deuce kissed her hard, "I am just happy you are alive. Let's get out of here and get you medicated. There are a whole bunch of law enforcement personnel at the compound waiting for you."

"I am so happy you came." Danica nodded vigorously. "How did you find me?"

"Grace, the stowaway girl you helped rescue, saw the picture of one of the men on a video Quade and I were watching, and she told us who he was."

"I guess we are even then," Danica gasped for breath, "I saved her life, and she saved mine because I think a couple more minutes struggling on this lonely road would probably end me."

Deuce looked at her, concerned. "Dani…"

"If I had my hiking bag, I could take some medication for this. I always have my epinephrine around."

"I carried your bag," Deuce said, "I had a hunch that you might need it. I also carried my med kit; either way, you are covered."

"You are handsome and smart," Danica murmured. "I have never had this so bad. What I had must have been the most potent milk I ever had."

"It will take just a few more minutes to get them, can you make it?"

Danica nodded and swiped her hand against her cheek, leaving long red welts on top of the ones that were already there.

"I heard that Leona Julius set this up. When we go back, she is going to have some explaining to do."

"No, she didn't," Danica muttered. "When Cyrus tore into Azaria about what she had done. She said it was her mother who called her, but while I was putting on my proper clothes in the dorm, Azaria apologized to me profusely.

She said that all of this was a genuine mistake, her brother called her and told her that I was being abused, and that it was a bad case, worse than when they were children. Whatever that means."

"They had a crappy childhood with their grandparents," Deuce shook his head. "It was pretty gruesome. I figured that Dale Julius told her that to stir up her sympathy, and she thought she had to act quickly. And when you were found, she couldn't blame her brother; she made her mother the fall guy."

"Leona's children dislike her, don't they?" Danica murmured. "I wonder what Dale thought would happen, that I would just disappear, and no one would care? What he did was pure evil."

"I agree." Deuce held on tighter to her hand as she stumbled. She was rapidly losing vision in the eye that had not yet swollen shut.

Deuce pulled her even closer to him. "I thought I lost contact with you when we were just texting each other, and it nearly drove me crazy. There was no hope of me letting you go after meeting you face to face and growing to love you."

Danica stopped and held on to his hand. "You really mean that? You love me?"

"More than I can say." Deuce looked at her solemnly. "I don't ever want to relive the last three days of horror I just went through."

"I love you too, DJ," Danica slurred her words, her lips were getting fat.

Deuce chuckled. "You look really bad. When we get home, and your face is back to its normal size, I am going to propose."

"And I'll say yes." Danica tried to smile. "I was thinking of a May wedding."

"That's two whole months away," Deuce said, "can you manage to wait that long?"

Danica nuzzled in his neck. "I'll manage, but only barely."

Deuce lifted her up. "Come on, I'll have to carry you."

"For the rest of your life?" Danica grinned.

"For the rest of my life," Deuce said fervently

Epilogue

Two months later

It was a beautiful garden wedding in Celia Jacksons' picturesque garden. The yellow and pink poui trees were in full bloom and they created a stunning backdrop for the wedding pictures. The bride wore a fitted ivory dress with a yellow flower behind her ear, and the groom looked dashing in navy blue.

They said their vows, had their first kiss as husband and wife and the family cheered giddily as they made their way down the makeshift center aisle that a yellow poui tree had carpeted with flowers.

"You next," Ace Senior said to Trey heartily.

Trey looked at his father and frowned. "I am the third one, remember? Trey means three. Two just got married, and One is not married yet. Your children are not doing this thing according to birth order."

"Yep, but Ace is getting married in December," Ace Senior said, "Deuce wasn't waiting. He was determined to tie the knot with his lady."

"They do make a beautiful couple," Trey said wistfully. "I am almost moved to tears by the beauty of it all."

"Don't mock the romance of the moment," Ace Senior said sternly. "I am going to find you a partner."

"I wasn't mocking the romance," Trey whispered fiercely. "And I will not be set up by my father. I am fine and stop going around and telling women that I am your only single son. I sound sad and depressed. I am quite fine. I am happy, ecstatic, delighted and blissfully single."

"I do these things because I have to help you out. You show no interest in any of the lovely ladies at church. I remember that you had a taste for strippers, ladies of the night, and women with questionable contacts with drug lords and kingpins and thugs."

Trey sighed. "I had a taste for one stripper. One. And I genuinely loved her, but that is all water under the bridge. I show no interest in anyone because I am a surgical resident, rushed off my feet at a busy hospital."

Ace senior chuckled. "You are single because you still have it bad for Kenya Kyle."

Trey looked at him in shock. "You know her real name?"

"I should," Ace Sr lost the grin on his face, "I had to find her official birth certificate to prove her age so that her pimp of a father wouldn't send you to jail."

Trey blanched.

"I also arranged for the young lady in question to escape from her life in the inner city. I don't think she would have made it alone after I dragged you out of the pit you two were living in and sent you to rehab."

"Now that's a mouthful," Trey murmured. "Once again,

I say, thank you, Dad for rescuing me from myself. I was different then."

"No thanks necessary," Ace Sr said, "just show that you have moved on from all of that by showing an interest in other people."

Trey wanted to comment that it was easier said than done but he didn't want to argue with his father.

Ace came over to them. "What are you two whispering so fiercely about? It is picture-taking time. Deuce wants one with just us three."

Trey got up in relief. "Remind me to never sit beside Dad at a wedding."

Ace grinned. "Dad, behave yourself."

Ace Senior winked. "For today."

Trey got a drink from a passing waiter. "Whatever happened to Dale Julius and his mom?"

"Leona left the island," Ace snorted, "She took the fall for Dale. She claimed that she orchestrated the whole thing and that Dale had nothing to do with it. She left Jamaica a month ago to go back to Canada. I don't think we'll be seeing her again.

"She gave up her bungalow at Golden Acres, and Dale sent a cheesy apology letter to Danica saying that he was sorry for the actions his mother took and that he would not bother her again. He hasn't so far, both Kelsey and Dale have backed off.

"As for the Machseh people who took Danica, they are charged with kidnapping. I don't know how that case will pan out."

"So the real perpetrator, Dale Julius is safe." Trey grumbled. "That doesn't seem fair does it?"

"Not fair." Ace murmured.

"Come on you two," Deuce said happily, "what are you looking so glum about?"

"In the gathering dusk, while he was giving his speech," Deuce stood up and looked at Danica.

"I am not one for long speeches. I would just like to quote my favorite song since meeting Danica online.

"I knew I loved you before I met you, I think I dreamed you into life…Forever and a day, Danica Jackson."

"Forever and a day," Danica blew him a kiss.

The End

Here is an excerpt from Trey
(The Jacksons Book 3)

The first time he went to a strip club he went to a bachelor party for his friend, Wayne. The second time he went alone to see her. He didn't sit at the dance area where the poles were, nor did he sit at the bar. He sat in the booth in the dark and watched as she sensually wound herself around a pole with a vacant look on her face.

Usually, there were five girls on the stage in the man cave lounge. Jaded had three lounges. The man cave was the place for the so-called tame viewer. There were no lap dances, the girls did not interact with the patrons, and they kept most of their skimpy clothes on.

"Technically they aren't strippers, just dancers," The friendly man at the door had said the first time he came into the semi dark room.

The man cave lounge was popular with couples and those attending bachelor parties. Go figure. Someone should analyze why that was, the tamest lounge had the most patrons. He wouldn't be the one to do any analyzing, though. His brain was tired, and he was slightly stoned, not high, just mellow. He had just taken his first-year med school exams, and he wanted to relax, and feel the buzz.

So here he was. In the dark. Watching her.

"So you like Angel, eh?" A gravelly-voiced man slid into his booth and asked. He looked like the boxer, George Foreman. "She's new."

Trey looked at him lazily. "There are five girls up there. How do you know which one I am looking at?"

"I've been watching you as you watch her. Your eyes are always on the left side of the stage. Besides, she looks like her name."

Trey snorted inelegantly. "They all look the same. Same wigs different colors, same moves, and same come hither looks designed to tantalize without any follow-ups."

The man laughed. "You sound bitter, but a money-man like you should never be. If you just come out of the darkness and go closer to the poles, I am sure all of them will be crawling over you like ants on honey. You are not bad looking either, that alone will have them flocking to you."

"A money-man." Trey laughed. "I am not a money-man, just a poor med student who just finished his exams."

"You are," the man murmured. "I can smell it on you. All of you well-to-do people smell alike."

"Like marijuana and Bleu De Chanel?" Trey turned back to the stage; he didn't like taking his eyes off her for long.

"No, like money and prestige." Tony guffawed. "Angel has the prettiest legs on the stage." The man said, a satisfied sound to his voice as if he had designed her legs himself. "And the best dancer's body. The only one who knows what she is really doing."

Trey narrowed his eyes at the man in the half-dark. "What are you, her pimp?"

"Pimp?" The man feigned shock. "Angel is not a sex worker, but if you want a date, I can arrange for you to meet her."

"If I want to meet her, I'll arrange it myself," Trey said stubbornly. "I don't want a middleman. What's your name again?"

"Tony Kyle, everybody calls me TK," The man said without hesitation. "I knew you were a good sort the moment I saw you. I hear how you speak when you ask for a drink, and I see you gravitating to the classiest girl here."

Trey was getting bored with the conversation and with

Tony. He just wanted to watch Angel.

Tony was right. She was undoubtedly the most interesting one to look at. She was lithe and toned and moved like there was some professional training behind her moves. She had the skin tone of powdered cinnamon and the sharp cheekbones of Naomi Campbell. She was truly outstanding.

At twenty-four, he considered himself a connoisseur where women were concerned, and this one, without having met her, had piqued his interest to the point of obsession.

It was such a pity that after this, he would go home to his empty apartment and drink himself to sleep.

He had finished his first year of med school and reasoned that he had earned the right to celebrate. He didn't want to celebrate alone. He wanted to celebrate with Angel.

"Here is her number," Tony said, sensing that he had zoned out of the conversation.

Trey took the number and looked at it. "What time does she get off?"

"In a half-hour," Tony said.

"Tell her to meet me by the black Mercedes in the parking lot," Trey said, "I don't particularly want to spend my night alone, and I am not paying for it. Got that?"

Tony grinned. "Got it."

Pryce Sisters Series

Baby For A Pryce (Book 1)- Giselle Pryce had a bright future, two scholarships from Ivy League schools and a track career that was going somewhere, when she discovered she was pregnant. She had several decisions to make.

Right Pryce Wrong Time (Book 2)- Tiana got her high school teacher James fired for inappropriate conduct because of her jealousy. When she meets him again as an adult in a different situation, she has no idea how to act.

Yours, For A Pryce (Book 3)- Toddy Pryce offers his favorite sister Elsa to his young political rival Mason Magnus in exchange to not run against him in the next elections.

Wiley Brothers Series

Between Brothers (Book 0)- The beginning of the Wiley brothers saga, Joseph Wiley's unconventional family life may prove to be fatal to some members of the family.

For Pete's Sake (Book 1)- Preston has a run in with a child named Pete who claims that he is the grandson of their former housekeeper Pamela Stone.

Crossing Jordan (Book 2)- Jordan is miffed when Shawn takes her new fiancé to Jamaica and insists that he be man of honor at their wedding.

Fire and Walter (Book 3)- Walter's past came rushing to greet him shortly after his appointment as church elder. The new pastor was his childhood molestor, his wife was his ex from college and her cousin was the girl who got away. Walter had a lot of decisions to make.

The Perfect Guy (Book 4) - After a patient five years waiting for Lucia, Guy had his work cut out for him to prove himself worthy of her affections. He had played the part of poor farmer for too long and now he had competition in the form of the handsome doctor Ace Jackson.

The Patience of A Saint (Book 5)- Something was wrong with Saint's wife Sandrene. It didn't take a genius to see that she was changed beyond all recognition. Saint had to get to the bottom of it, before it was too late for them to salvage anything from the relationship.

A Case of Love (Book 6)- After a concert, Case is offered a girl to buy. Her fate was in his hands. He could keep her or leave her to the mercy of her evil family.

Resetter Series

Never Too Late (Book 1)- Addi finds out she is a resetter and goes back to the summer of 92 to change her family's lives.

Never Say Never (Book 2)- Skyler's handsome college lecturer, who happens to be her neighbor, has a 't' in his palms. Should she tell him the significance of it. If she does, would he believe her?

Now or Never (Book 3)- Ten years later Addi and Randy meet again at Randy's engagement party. Why is it that the chemistry between them was still so potent? Can they ever have a future together? Would Randy choose her this time around?

Almost Never (Book 4)- Tech genius Joshua Porter had all but given up on love. He then meets Portia, an inmate at the female penitentiary and his life takes a turn for the adventurous.

The Scarlett Family Series

Scarlett Baby (Book 1)- When the head of the Scarlett family died, Yuri had to return home to Treasure Beach for the funeral. What he didn't count on was seeing Marla, his childhood sweetheart and his best friend's wife. And when emotions overwhelm them and a few months later Marla is pregnant, Yuri wants the impossible: his best friend's wife and the baby they made together...

Scarlett Sinner (Book 2)- Pastor Troy Scarlett realizes the hard way that some sins are bound to be revealed, like the child that he had out of wedlock with his wife's mortal enemy from college. His wife Chelsea was not happy with the status quo. She was not taking care of the son of the woman she had so despised from college. And she could not get over the deep betrayal that she felt from her husband's indiscretion.

Scarlett Secret (Book 3)- Terri Scarlett had a soft spot for her friend, Lola. She was funny and sweet and they looked remarkably alike. But when Lola's Arab prince demands his bride, Terri foolishly exchange places with her friend and they meet up on a world of trouble.

***Scarlett Love (Book 4)*-** Slater always looked forward to delivering packages to the law firm where he could get a glimpse of the stunning female lawyer, Amoy Gardener. Unfortunately, for Slater a woman like Amoy would not take him seriously, especially when she found out that he could not read!

***Scarlett Promise (Book 5)*-** Driven by desperation Lisa Barclay decides to make some extra money by prostituting herself after being kicked out in the streets. Her first customer turns out to be a popular government senator and then to her horror he dies...

***Scarlett Bride (Book 6)*-** When Oliver Scarlett's missionary work in the Congo region was coming to an end, he had a decision to make, marry Ashaki Azanga and save her from being the fourth wife to the chief of the village or leave her to her fate and get on with his life...

***Scarlett Heart (Book 7)*-** After receiving a heart transplant shy librarian Noah Scarlett started to take on character traits that were unlike him and he kept dreaming of a girl named Cassandra Green...

Rebound Series

***On The Rebound*-** For Better or Worse, Brandon vowed to stay with Ashley, but when worse got too much he moved out and met Nadine. For the first time in years he felt happy, but then Ashley remembered her wedding vows...

***On The Rebound 2*-** Ashley reinvented herself and was now a first lady in a country church in Primrose Hill, but her obsessed ex friend Regina showed up and started digging into the lives of the saints at church. Somebody didn't like Regina's digging. Someone had secrets that were shocking enough to kill for...

Magnolia Sisters

Dear Mystery Guy (Book 1)- Della Gold details her life in a journal dedicated to a mystery guy. But when fascination turns into obsession she finds herself wanting to learn even more about him but in her pursuit of the mystery guy she begins to learn more about herself...

Bad Girl Blues (Book 2)- Brigid Manderson wanted to go to med school but for the time being she was an escort working for her mother, an ex-prostitute. When her latest customer offers her the opportunity of a lifetime would she take it? Or would she choose the harder path and uncertain love with a Christian guy?

Her Mistaken Dreams (Book 3)- Caitlin Denvers dream guy had serious issues. He has a dead wife in his past and he was the main suspect in her murder. Did he really do it? Or did Caitlin for the first time have a mistaken dream?

Just Like Yesterday (Book 4)- Hazel Brown lost six months of memory including the summer that she conceived her son, and had no idea who his father could be. Now that she had the means to fight to get him back from the Deckers, she finds out that the handsome Curtis Decker is willing to share her son with her after all.

New Song Series

Going Solo (Book 1)- Carson Bell, had a lovely voice, a heart of gold, and was no slouch in the looks department. So why did Alice abandon him and their daughter? What did she want after ten years of silence?

Duet on Fire (Book 2)- Ian and Ruby had problems trying to conceive a child. If that wasn't enough, her ex-lover the current pastor of their church wants her back...

Tangled Chords (Book 3)- Xavier Bell, the poor, ugly duckling has made it rich and his looks have been incredibly improved too. Farrah Knight, hotel heiress had cruelly rejected him in the past but now she needed help. Could Xavier forgive and forget?

Broken Harmony(Book 4)- Aaron Lee, wanted the top job in his family company but he had a moral clause to consider just when Alka, his married ex-girlfriend walks back into his life.

A Past Refrain (Book 5)- Jayce had issues with forgetting Haley Greenwald even though he had a new woman in his life. Will he ever be able to shake his love for Haley?

Perfect Melody (Book 6)- Logan Moore had the perfect wife, Melody but his secretary Sabrina was hell bent on breaking up the family. Sabrina wanted Logan whatever the cost and she had a secret about Melody, that could shatter Melody's image to everyone.

The Bancroft Family Series

Homely Girl (Book 0) - April and Taj were opposites in so many ways. He was the cute, athletic boy that everybody wanted to be friends with. She was the overweight, shy, and withdrawn girl. Do April and Taj have a love that can last a lifetime? Or will time and separate paths rip them apart?

Saving Face (Book 1) - Mount Faith University drama begins with a dead president and several suspects including the president in waiting Ryan Bancroft.

Tattered Tiara (Book 2) - Micah Bancroft is targeted by femme fatale Deidra Durkheim. There are also several rape cases to be solved.

Private Dancer (Book 3) Adrian Bancroft was gutted when he returned to Jamaica and found out that his first and only love Cathy Taylor was a stripper and was literally owned by the menacing drug lord, Nanjo Jones.

Goodbye Lonely (Book 4) - Kylie Bancroft was shy and had to resort to going to confidence classes. How could she win the love of Gareth Beecher, her faculty adviser, a man with a jealous ex-wife in his past and a current mystery surrounding a hand found in his garden?

Practice Run (Book 5) - Marcus Bancroft had many reasons to avoid Mount Faith but Deidra Durkheim was not one of them. Unfortunately, on one of his visits he was the victim of a deliberate hit and run.

Sense of Rumor (Book 6) - Arnella Bancroft was the wild, passionate Bancroft, the creative loner who didn't mind living dangerously; but when a terrible thing happened to her at her friend Tracy's party, it changed her. She found that courting rumors can be devastating and that only the truth could set her free.

A Younger Man (Book 7)- Pastor Vanley Bancroft loved Anita Parkinson despite their fifteen-year age gap, but Anita had a secret, one that she could not reveal to Vanley. To tell him would change his feelings toward her, or force him to give up the ministry that he loved so much.

Just To See Her (Book 8)- Jessica Bancroft had the opportunity to meet her fantasy guy Khaled, he was finally coming to Mount Faith but she had feelings for Clay Reid, a guy who had all the qualities she was looking for. Who would she choose and what about the weird fascination Khaled had for Clay?

The Three Rivers Series

Private Sins (Book 1)- Kelly, the first lady at Three Rivers Church was pregnant for the first elder of her church. Could she keep the secret from her husband and pretend that all was well?

Loving Mr. Wright (Book 2)- Erica saw one last opportunity to ditch her single life when Caleb Wright appeared in her town. He was perfect for her, but what was he hiding?

Unholy Matrimony (Book 3) - Phoebe had a problem, she was poor and unhappy. Her solution to marry a rich man was derailed along the way with her feelings for Charles Black, the poor guy next door.

If It Ain't Broke (Book 4)- Chris Donahue wanted a place in his child's life. Pinky Black just wanted his love. She also wanted him to forget his obsession with Kelly and love her. That shouldn't be so hard? Should it?

Contemporary Romance/Drama

After The End--Torn between two lovers. Colleen married her high school sweetheart, Isaiah, hoping that they would live happily ever after but life intruded and Isaiah disappeared at sea. She found work with the rich and handsome, Enrique Lopez, as a housekeeper and realized that she couldn't keep him at arms length...

Love Triangle: Three Sides To The Story- George, the husband, Marie, the wife and Karen-the mistress. They all get to tell their side of the story.

The Preacher And The Prostitute - Prostitution and the clergy don't mix. Tell that to ex-prostitute, Maribel, who finds herself in love with the Pastor at her church. Can an ex-prostitute and a pastor have a future together?

New Beginnings - Inner city girl Geneva was offered an opportunity of a lifetime when she found out that her 'real' father was a very wealthy man. Her decision to live uptown meant that she had to leave Froggie, her 'ghetto don,' behind. She also found herself battling with her stepmother and battling her emotions for Justin, a suave up-towner.

Full Circle- After graduating from university, Diana

wanted to return to Jamaica to find her siblings. What she didn't foresee was that she would meet Robert Cassidy and that both their pasts would be intertwined, and that disturbing questions would pop up about their parentage, just when they were getting close.

Historical Fiction/Romance

The Empty Hammock- Workaholic, Ana Mendez, fell asleep in a hammock and woke up in the year 1494. It was the time of the Tainos, a time when life seemed simpler, but Ana knew that all of that was about to change.

The Pull Of Freedom- Even in bondage the people, freshly arrived from Africa, considered themselves free. Led by Nanny and Cudjoe the slaves escaped the Simmonds' plantation and went in different directions to forge their destiny in the new country called Jamaica.

Jamaican Comedy (Material contains Jamaican dialect)

Di Taxi Ride And Other Stories- Di Taxi Ride and Other Stories is a collection of twelve witty and fast paced short stories. Each story tells of a unique slice of Jamaican life.

Made in the USA
Monee, IL
21 February 2021